# Domain Expeditionary Force
# Rescue Mission

**by**

**Lawrence R. Spencer**

**A Science Fiction Story**

based on the Top Secret transcripts published in the book

"*Alien Interview*"

# DISCLAIMER:

## THIS BOOK IS A SCIENCE FICTION STORY.

**The premise and characters in this book is based on the facts and ideas presented in the factual, non-fiction book 'Alien Interview', edited by Lawrence R. Spencer**

**This book is in no way factual, nor is intended to represent any factual information whatsoever. This book is a contrivance of the imagination of the author. This book was written at the suggestion of Eric Pham who wanted to create a motion picture film script based on the ideas and premises of the non-fiction book, Alien Interview.**

**This book is a work of fiction only, and it not to be interpreted otherwise by the reader.**

**Lawrence R. Spencer**

**Author**

**2013**

# Domain Expeditionary Force
## Rescue Mission



Cover and book design by Lawrence R. Spencer

Printed in the United States of America
First Edition Printing: 2013

ISBN:

# ABOUT THE INSIDE COVER ART SYMBOLISM

The cover art symbolizes the presence and activities surrounding Earth of a secret, intergalactic society called The Brothers of The Serpent (BOTS).

This powerful remnant of the Old Empire has been using Earth as a prison planet for at least 30,000 years. Immortal Spiritual Beings (IS-BEs) are being transported from all over this and neighboring galaxies, as "untouchable" or undesirable persons, and illegally imprisoned on Earth inside biological bodies.

The BOTS set up false façade civilizations on Earth as a trick to prevent IS-BEs from remembering their true origins. The BOTS maintain electronic detection devices, or *AQERTs, throughout this end of the galaxy to capture any IS-BE, who, on body death, may attempt to leave this region of space.

According to the top secret transcripts published in the book, *Alien Interview*, a base in the Himalayas housing a battalion of 3,000 alien invaders from the Domain Expeditionary Force (DEF) was destroyed in a surprise attack by forces of the Old Empire under the direction of the (BOTS).

The members of the DEF battalion were given amnesia, along with all the other "untouchable" inmates on Earth, and have remained captive. In 5,965 BCE the DEF sent a group of missionaires to Earth to locate and rescue the members of their lost battalion. This task proved more formidable and treacherous than anyone could have imagined.

The winged serpents or dragons are the emblem of the Brothers of The Snake (BOTS). This is a symbol commonly found in nearly all of the ancient societies of Earth in various forms.

The star symbolizes the extraterrestrial power of the BOTS, who are the "gods" of Egypt and other ancient false façade civilizations. Priests of various Earth religions unwittingly assist them to maintain control through superstition and lies hypnotically implanted in the human population by the BOTS operation.

The circle within the star represents the planet Mars.

The jewel within the circle represents the hidden, underground base of operations of the BOTS which administer remote, hypnotic mind-control activities used to monitor the inmate population on Earth.

The chalice, or grail, is a symbol of the AQERTS which capture the spiritual essence of all IS-BEs on Earth, including the members of the lost DEF battalion, and hold them in a perpetual state of amnesia and imprisonment inside of biological bodies.

The symbol inside the chalice represents the IS-BEs of Earth, including those of the captured DEF battalion.

The prison planet Earth is encircled by the tails, or electronic force screens, of the BOTS that prevent IS-BEs from escaping.

* *AQERT*:  Literally, Egyptian name for "the abode of the dead".

# PREAMBLE

*"Once the IS-BEs expelled from the "Old Empire" arrived on Earth, they were given amnesia, and hypnotically tricked into thinking that something else had happened to them.*

*The next step was to implant the IS-BEs into biological bodies on Earth. The bodies became the human populations of "false civilizations" which were designed and installed in the minds of IS-BEs to look completely unlike the "Old Empire".*

*All of the IS-BEs of India, Egypt, Babylon, Greece, Rome, and Medieval Europe were guided to pattern and build the cultural elements of these societies based on standard patterns developed by the IS-BEs of many earlier, similar civilizations on "Sun Type 12, Class 7" planets that have existed for trillions of years throughout the universe."*

-- excerpted from Top Secret government interview transcripts published in the book, "Alien Interview"

---

*"Through clever and constant application of propaganda, people can be made to see paradise as hell, and also the other way round, to consider the most wretched sort of life as paradise."* -- Adolph Hitler (20 April 1889 – 30 April 1945)

---

*The evil of the world is made possible by nothing but the sanction you give it."* -- Ayn Rand (January 20, 1905 – March 6, 1982)

---

*"When you think of the long and gloomy history of man, you will find more hideous crimes have been committed in the name of obedience than have ever been committed in the name of rebellion."* -- C. P. Snow (15 October 1905–1 July 1980)

---

*"Man is equally incapable of seeing the nothingness from which he emerges and the infinity in which he is engulfed."* -- Blaise Pascal (1623 - 1662)

---

*"We are the people our parents warned us about."*
- Jimmy Buffett (December 25, 1946 -- )

# FOREWORD

*"There are several obvious reasons that The Domain, and other space civilizations do not land on Earth or make their presence known. It takes a very brave IS-BE to come down through the atmosphere and land on Earth, because it is a prison planet, with a very uncontrolled, psychotic population. And, no IS-BE is entirely proof against the risk of entrapment, as with the members of The Domain Expeditionary Force who were captured in the Himalayas 8,200 years ago."*

-- Excerpted from the Official Transcript of the U.S. Army Air Force Roswell Army Air Field, 509th Bomb Group:

SUBJECT: ALIEN INTERVIEW, 26. 7. 1947, 1st Session published in the book *Alien Interview,* edited by Lawrence R. Spencer, 2008.

# DEDICATION

**This book is dedicated to Matilda O'Donnell MacElroy, who has been rescued by and returned to active duty with the Domain Expeditionary Force.**

**May we all remember our true origins and recover the inherent spiritual abilities that are who we really are.**

# TABLE OF CONTENTS

**DISCLAIMER: ........ 2**

ABOUT THE INSIDE COVER ART SYMBOLISM ........ 4
PREAMBLE ........ 7
FOREWORD ........ 9
DEDICATION ........ 11
TABLE OF CONTENTS ........ 13

**A MESSAGE FROM MATILDA ........ 17**

COPY OF THE E-MAIL RECEIVED ........ 19
THE "ATTACHED DOCUMENT" ........ 22
DEF NOMENCLATURE NOTICE ........ 23

**DEF PERSONNEL REORIENTATION MANUAL ........ 27**

DEF P.R. MANUAL, SECTION ONE: ........ 28
PREREQUISITE CRITERIA FOR RESCUE FROM EARTH ........ 28
SEQUENCE OF PERSONAL RECOGNITION ........ 28
DEF P.R. MANUAL, SECTION TWO: ........ 29
DIFFERENCES BETWEEN EARTH AND THE DOMAIN ........ 33
1) PHYSICAL UNIVERSE SURVIVAL VS.. THE IS-BE ........ 34
2) PHYSICAL UNIVERSE IS-BE BEHAVIOR VS. DOMAIN IS-BE BEHAVIOR. 40
3) GAMES VS. ALL-MOTHER ........ 43
4) PHYSICAL UNIVERSE TIME VS. DOMAIN TIME ........ 46
5) AMNESIA VS. MEMORY ........ 52
6) PLANETARY ENVIRONMENTS VS. IS-BE UNIVERSES ........ 55
7) IS-BE VS. BODY ........ 58
8) TECHNOLOGY OF ENTRAPMENT ........ 64
9) INTENTIONAL CHAOS VS. BENEVOLENT CONTROL ........ 71
10) LANGUAGE VS. IS-BE COMMUNICATION ........ 74
11) THE TREE OF LIFE VS. PSIONICS ........ 76
12) SENSATION: PERCEPTION VS. CREATION ........ 84

**REORIENTATION BRIEFING FOR REACTIVATED DEF PERSONNEL ........ 91**

PART ONE: PRINCIPLE OF ALL-MOTHER ........ 93
THE ESSENTIAL NATURE OF UNIVERSES ........ 97
PART TWO: THE ETERNALLY BENEVOLENT DOMAIN ........ 102
PART THREE: THE DOMAIN EXPEDITIONARY FORCE ........ 106
PART FOUR: DEF MISSION 162589 SYNOPSIS ........ 108
WE CREATE THE ETERNALLY BENEVOLENT DOMAIN!PART FIVE: MISSION 162589.32 ........ 112
I. ROLL CALL: ........ 114
PERSONNEL OFFICER "LOR-EL" (LOR-EL) ........ 114
REGIONAL COMMANDER "RAZAR" (RAH-ZAHR) ........ 114

Officer, Pilot, Engineer "Airl" (air-el) .... 115
Aquatic Unit Mission Specialist "Lemore" (leh-more) .... 115
Land Mission Specialist "Rameth" (rah-meth) .... 116
Aerial Mission Specialist "Lathor" (lah-thor) .... 117
Communications Specialist, "Hezmel" (hez-meal) .... 117
Therapeutic Specialist, "Lam-Mantra" (lahm-mahn-trah) .... 118
Medical Officer, 1st Grade, "Raal-laam" (rahl-lahm) .... 118
II. CLASSIFICATION .... 120
Mission Code Name: "Prison Break" .... 120
III. MISSION EXECUTION .... 121
A. Restated Mission Statement .... 121
B. Restated Commander's Intent .... 122
Subsection 1 -- Mission Data: Supplemental .... 123
PROTOCOL VIOLATION REPORT 1434 .... 123
C. Mission Debrief Narrative .... 126
D. Mission Background Information .... 134
(1) Supplemental reconnaissance .... 137
(2) BOTS origins and organization .... 139
(3) AQERT operation and location .... 141
E. Serpent Symbols .... 145
Summary Observation of BOTS Behavior .... 147

**DEBRIEF, SECTION TWO: HISTORICAL SUMMARY .... 148**

PERIOD 1: MISSION OPERATIONS .... 148
PRISON PLANET .... 148
FALSE FACADE CIVILIZATIONS .... 148
PRISON GUARDS .... 152
DETERRENTS TO DEF PERSONNEL RECOVERY .... 158
THE BOTS PRISON PLANET ADMINISTRATION .... 163
AQERT EFFECTIVENESS .... 170
PERIOD 2: MISSION OPERATIONS .... 173
DEF BASES .... 173
PERIOD 3: ACTIVE WARFARE .... 176
RAVANA VIMANAS BY AIR .... 176
MOSES ON THE MOUNTAIN .... 179
PERIOD 4: A VICTORY .... 188
PERIOD 5: CYRUS, THE GREAT .... 194
PERIOD 6: REINFORCEMENTS AND RENAISSANCE .... 196
PERIOD 7: DEF OFFICER TESLA .... 203
PERIOD 8: MARS, CYDONIA BASE .... 207
PERIOD 9: PRISON PLANET .... 211
PERIOD 10: ROSWELL REVELATION .... 214

**YOUR LIFE IN THE DEF .... 216**

DUTIES AND REGIMEN .... 216
LIFESTYLE AND LIBERTIES .... 218
Quarters And Facilities .... 218
The Imaginearium .... 219

THE LOUNGE ........ 220
THE ARCHIVE ........ 220
VEHICLES AND EXCURSIONS ........ 221
**THE DOMAIN ANNEXATION OF EARTH ........ 222**
**CONCLUSION ........ 224**
**PERSONAL NOTE FROM ADEET- REN ........ 225**
INDEX ........ 231

# A MESSAGE FROM MATILDA

On Tuesday, December 15, 2009 I received a very unusual and unexpected e-mail. At first, I thought it was sent as a prank. Usually, I wouldn't look past the Subject line before deleting it. But, as I quickly skimmed the body of the message the words "DEF Mission" jumped out at me, so I kept reading. After scanning it for viruses, I opened the text document that was attached.

Anyone who has read the book "Alien Interview" knows that I received letters, notes and Top Secret US military transcripts of in 2007 as part of the "dying request" of an old woman I had spoken to on the phone only once, 10 years earlier. Her request was that I make them known to as many people as possible.

At that time Matilda O'Donnell MacElroy was living in Ireland, where she passed away a few months later. She served as a nurse at the US Army Air Force 509th Bomb Group in Roswell, N.M. in 1947. When the famous "Roswell Incident" happened, she was the person assigned to conduct a series of telepathic interviews with the lone surviving alien pilot of the crashed "flying disc".

Since July of 2008, when the book was published, I have done my best to let people know about the transcripts. I gave permission to have a PDF version of the book made available free of charge, knowing that once a digital copy of the book was published that it would spread all over the internet.

Along with the "help" of Google, which steals and publishes every book ever printed, as well as hundreds of "bit-torrent" websites that pirate copyrighted material with unabashed abandon, and several internet radio show interviews I gave to explain how I came by the material, the book has spread like a viral pandemic.

I put up a website for the book (www.alieninterview.org) and started writing a Blog to speculate about the events and phenomena described in the transcripts.

It's difficult to know exactly how many people have read the book. But an educated guess, judging from the number of websites, chat rooms, blogs, forums and reproductions that come up in various key word searches, a safe estimate would be that at least 100,000 so far.

For those who are still interested in the material, regardless of whether or not they "believe" that the material is "fact" or "fiction", I am publishing the content of the e-mail and the attachment I received, in its exact, unaltered (except for formatting) form.

I don't think this material needs any further introduction or explanation from me. So, I'm publishing these documents, as requested of me by "Adeet-Ren", formerly identified on Earth as Matilda O'Donnell MacElroy:

*"...to those few who are willing to look and think for themselves, to discover possible solutions to the dilemma of being imprisoned on a planet and kept in a perpetual state of amnesia and chaos...".*

And like "Adeet-Ren", who has lately returned to active duty as a member of the Domain Expeditionary Force :

*"It is the most sincere desire of The Domain that all IS-BEs of Earth will eventually be recovered to their natural spiritual state of independence, power and immortality...".*

I think the Alien Interview transcripts make it clear that if we're ever going to escape from our imprisonment on Earth, we're going to have get busy doing it ourselves.

Eternity is in the future. And right now eternity doesn't look like a very pleasant place to be headed.

As Matilda once said, "Good Luck to All of Us".

# COPY OF THE E-MAIL RECEIVED

---

**From:** Matilda MacElroy <defbase33co07@gmail.com>

**Date:** Sun, January 24, 2010 11:25 am

**To:** Lawrence R. Spencer <info@alieninterview.org>

**Subject:** DEF Mission Debrief

Dear Lawrence,

Before you destroy this message, please read the attached document entitled, "DEF Mission Debrief". I assure you that, once you have finished reading the document, you will understand that this is a legitimate communication from me.

Since I mailed you the Top Secret US Army Air Force transcripts of my interviews with the Domain Expeditionary Force Officer, Pilot and Engineer, "Air", I have been informed that you did, indeed, publish the transcripts and my notes, exactly as you received them from me, in the form of a book.

Please accept my most grateful and sincere thanks for having gone to all of the time and trouble to do this. I understand that the book has been distributed freely on the communications network, and that it has been received with a good deal of interest by tens of thousands of readers. Of course, as expected, the majority of people on Earth will never be interested or notice it.

However, I am sending you this document to relay to those few who are willing to look and think for themselves, to discover possible solutions to the dilemma of being imprisoned on a planet and kept in a perpetual state of chaos and amnesia by The Brothers of The Serpent.

I have received authorization from my superior officers at the DEF Base to send this information to you. Ordinarily, such a communication would be absolutely forbidden and prevented by standard DEF procedure, which is to avoid contact with IS-BEs on Earth, unless it is a part of our mission to recover the 3,000 members of the DEF battalion that we attacked, captured, given amnesia and sent back to Earth to inhabit bodies by the Brothers of The Serpent prison operators.

As you have correctly assumed by now, I have the very good fortune of having been "rescued" from Earth by the DEF Mission of which Officer, Pilot and Engineer "Airl" is a member. I was unable to disclose a detailed description of my relationship with the DEF in the package I sent to you from Ireland. However, now that I have left my former body, as Matilda O'Donnell MacElroy, and returned to active duty with The Domain Expeditionary Force, I feel that it is appropriate to reveal more detailed information to you, and anyone else who may be interested.

As before, I am asking you to publish the attached document in its unaltered entirety. It is understood that very few people on Earth will read it. However, the DEF Mission which has been stationed in this solar system since 5965 BCE, in search of the 3,000 members of the DEF "lost battalion", has been terminated and it's personnel will soon be recalled to the DEF Central Command Outpost for re-assignment to other duties, or to receive new orders regarding the disposition of our lost personnel.

I am sending you the attached document in the hope that some members of the "lost battalion" may read it, and in so doing, "remember" that they are not natives of the Old Empire, of Earth, or of the physical universe. Every member of the Domain Expeditionary Force is extremely valuable to us.

However, the DEF encountered extraordinary difficulties in contacting and recovering these lost personnel from Earth. This is due entirely to the amnesia / thought control mechanisms installed around Earth to ensure that it remains a secret prison planet under the control of the Brothers of The Serpent. As you will learn from the attached document, the DEF has exhausted the resources and technology available to The Domain in this sector of this galaxy at this time.

The DEF will continue to use Space Station 33 as a base of operation for targets related to The Domain Expeditionary Force Invasion Plan. However, whether or not a renewed search for our lost personnel on Earth will ever become practical is not know at this time.

If any members of the lost battalion should read this document and wish to be contacted by the DEF, they have only to remember their true identity and "think" the thought. Meanwhile, as far as I am aware, the inmates of Earth are left to their own ingenuity and integrity to solve the problem of escaping from prison planet Earth.

It is the most sincere desire of The Domain that all IS-BEs of Earth will eventually be recovered to their natural spiritual state of independence, power and immortality, as embodied in the Eternally Benevolent Domain, by the principle of "All-Mother, and in the entity of "The Omniscient and Omnipotent Matriarch".

Your Eternal Friend,

"Adeet-Ren", a.k.a. Matilda O'Donnell MacElroy

Communication Authorization DEFMO162589.32 - 24, Medical Officer, 1st Grade, "Raal-laam", Domain Expeditionary Force, PERSONNEL RECOVERY MISSION, Rest-Care-Cure Unit, Galaxy 3793, Sun 12, Space Station 33, Asteroid Belt

Transmission Authorization DEFCO07MO162589.32 - 49, Domain Expeditionary Force Communications Officer 07, "Hezmel", DEF INVASION FORCE: MISSION 162589, Galaxy 3793, Sun 12, Space Station 33

# THE "ATTACHED DOCUMENT"

The document which follows, entitled, "DEF Mission Debrief ", is reproduced as received by me, with formatting changed required for publication in the form of a book.

As no footnotes or comments are needed, the only alteration to the original text file I received was to format the fonts, headings, page and margin sizes to make them "prettier" and to conform with the printing requirements of the publisher.

-- Lawrence R. Spencer, Editor

# DEF NOMENCLATURE NOTICE

The following information has been translated as accurately as possible into the Earth language, "North American English", circa 2.0394 DEF Mission Cycles (**Note**: One DEF Mission Cycle = 5,000 Earth Solar years)

Earth Solar Date/Time: 2455119.2203588

All communications included in this transmission have been transcribed from telepathic communications between officers and personnel of DEF MISSION 162589.32.

All communications are encoded in the Universal Domain Invasion Nomenclature, version 163.256.598, for transmission to Domain Expeditionary Force Headquarters, Universal Sector 29, Spatial Grid Section 498 / 237 / 698, with the exception of three terms: "IS-BE", "Domain" and "Omnitheistic"

A word that accurately defines the concept of a personal, immortal, spiritual entity is not native to any known Earth language. Because Earth inhabitants are held in a perpetual state of amnesia, they no longer recall or perceive themselves as eternal spiritual entities. Therefore, the following definition is contrived and applied to the term "IS-BE":

> *"**IS-BE**" = the primary nature of an immortal being is that they live in a timeless state of "is", and the only reason for their existence is that they decide to "be".*

Unfortunately, this definition does not include a description of the graduated scale of ability, mobility, understanding and power of an "IS-BE" that is commonly understood by citizens of The Eternally Benevolent Domain.

The nature of an IS-BE from The Domain is fundamentally unique, and does not share the peculiar features of IS-BEs who collectively create and sustain the Physical Universe. The universes of The Domain do not contain physical attributes, such as particles of solid energy or objects located in a space / time continuum.

"**Domain**" = The incomplete interpretation of the word "Domain" as a descriptive term for our civilization is supplemented by a more accurate and complete definition with the phrase *"The Eternally Benevolent Domain",* under the guidance of **"***The Omniscient and Omnipotent Matriarch"* (abbrev: Omnimat) in accordance with the principle of *"All-Mother".*

"**Omnitheistic**" = The philosophic principle that observes that every IS-BE is a "god". The primary differences in god-like ability or power between one IS-BE and another have to do with magnitude and a uniquely individual point of view.

In keeping with the principle of "All-Mother", it is been observed that all universes are the creation of one or more IS-BEs, individually or in collaboration with or against other IS-BEs. All life-forms, not matter how varied, are conceived, created and animated by IS-BEs.

Each IS-BE creates all that it perceives, but does not necessarily care to perceive all that is has created. The behavior of selectively choosing not to be responsible for one's own creation, alteration or destruction of a universe, or any part of it leads to the persistence of universes, which is called time.

The notion that there is only "one" god, as in monotheism, or that there are only a few gods who are responsible for the creation and causation of universes, as in pantheism, is an attempt by an IS-BE to deny responsibility for oneself and for one's own creations. Such denials do not alter the fundamental nature or ability of an IS-BE, and confirms that an IS-BE is the source of all perception.

The philosophical premise of "Omnitheism" is defined as the observation that all IS-BEs are gods. There are as many "gods", in number, quality and order of magnitude of power, as there are Immortal Spiritual Beings.

**WE CREATE THE ETERNALLY BENEVOLENT DOMAIN!**

Attested:

Domain Expeditionary Force Communications Officer 07, "Hezmel", DEF INVASION FORCE: MISSION 162589, Galaxy 3793, Sun 12, Space Station 33

# DEF PERSONNEL REORIENTATION MANUAL

**Reorientation of "Lost Battalion" Personnel Adeet-Ren***

Compiled by

Medical Officer, 1st Grade, "Raal-Laam"

Domain Expeditionary Force

PERSONNEL RECOVERY MISSION

Rest-Care-Cure Unit

Galaxy 3793, Sun 12, Space Station 33, Asteroid Belt

*The DEF personnel name for Matilda O'Donnell MacElroy is "Adeet-Ren" (pronounced: in N.A.E. as "add-eat-wren")

**DEF P.R. MANUAL, SECTION ONE:**

## PREREQUISITE CRITERIA FOR RESCUE FROM EARTH

**NOTE:** *Although the best efforts of DEF Missionaires have produced a few successful rescues, as noted in the attached debrief, the DEF discovered that the following actions must be taken by any IS-BE, on their own volition, in order for any rescue assistance to be effective, as follow:*

**SEQUENCE OF PERSONAL RECOGNITION**

- The first step is to discover that your are an IS-BE.
- Next, discover that your are a prisoner.
    1) as an IS-BE in a biological body, and
    2) as an inmate on a prison planet
- Remember that you came to Earth from another planet, galaxy or universe. (The exact origin point and date of arrival on Earth should be established precisely.)
- Decide whether you want to escape from Earth, or remain imprisoned in perpetuity.

If you choose to escape from Earth, please continue reading the remainder of these materials. If not, any further assistance to you by The Domain is impossible.

**DEF P.R. MANUAL, SECTION TWO:**

SUMMARY OF RECOVERY AND REORIENTATION OF DEF LOST BATTALION MEMBER: Adeet-Ren

Shortly after your first encounter with Officer, Pilot and Engineer Airl at the Roswell US Army Air Force Base where you were stationed as a Flight Nurse in 1947, you became increasing aware that there was far more to your relationship, and to your existence, than was initially apparent.

As recounted in the your notes, and the military transcripts of the interviews with Airl, the first recollections of your previous relationship with The Domain began when you realized that you could communicate telepathically with Airl. This revelation, by itself, was enough to startle you out of the haze of amnesia in which you had been held captive on Earth for nearly 10,000 years.

Although the realization of direct spirit-to-spirit communication may have been shocking and dramatic, after 10,000 years of human oblivion, it was not enough, in itself, to awaken you from your hypnotic sleep. The communication you began with Airl in 1947 was continued over the following 60 years of your life on Earth, and improved steadily during that time.

Since then you have learned that recovering the lost memory of one's own identity, after having undergone the electronic shock and hypnotic "treatments" secretly and forcefully administered by the Brothers of The Serpent, seemed nearly impossible. In fact, to date, only a few of the Officers, pilots, specialists and support personnel from the 3,000 member DEF Battalion who were murdered, captured and incarcerated on Earth for 10,000 years have been recovered to active duty. You are one of the fortunate few who have returned to active duty with the DEF.

Considering that DEF Mission162589.32 has been deployed in a full-time effort to locate and recover your compatriots for more than 1.5946 mission cycle, since 5,965 BCE, you may consider yourself very, very fortunate indeed. Had it not been for the very unusual circumstances of the crash of the craft piloted by Officer Airl at Roswell, it is very likely that you would still be inhabiting a humanoid body on Earth rather than enjoying your freedom and responsibilities, once again, as a member of the DEF.

As you know, you are currently stationed on the DEF base in the asteroid field which is part of the installations of Space Station 33 in the solar system surrounding Earth. The communication you are reading now has been translated into North American English by Communications Officer 07, "Hezmel", with whom you have become acquainted since your return to active duty. She is also assisting you to recovery your IS-BE memory which was so greatly impaired while on Earth. Since Hezmel has been a communications specialist for billions of years, she is very well acquainted with thousands of indigenous languages and cultures across the vast space controlled by The Domain.

According to the account of your initial meeting, in the debrief provided to the DEF by Officer Airl, the first "words" or impressions that you understood were the answers the following questions during those interviews:

> "*'What type of society do you have?'*, to which Officer Airl replied, "ORDER. POWER. FUTURE ALWAYS. CONTROL. GROW."
>
> The next question asked was, *'Are there other intelligent life forms besides yourself in the universe?'*
>
> Officer Airl replied, "EVERYWHERE. WE ARE GREATEST / HIGHEST OF ALL."

In retrospect, after more than 60 years of continued communication with Airl, and other members of the DEF rescue mission, you have recovered a much more complete understanding of her answers to these questions about The Domain.

These interviews were published on Earth after your "death", or departure from the body in 2008. Thankfully, the transcripts and notes, and comments you provided were duplicated the faithfully, so it is not necessary for me to make any comments or corrections concerning that material.

Now the "Pandora's box" has been opened on Earth to reveal the truth behind many of the secrets under which the IS-BEs on

Earth exist, it is now necessary, in order to enhance your recovery, to share a much more complete, and detailed description of The Domain with you. Please read this material, as it will help you to regain your memory of who you really are and where you came from.

The DEF Mission has discovered that one of the fundamental aids to memory recovery is to review images, and information about the past, both on Earth and before you came to Earth.

Now that you have returned to active duty with the DEF, the faint outlines you regained through your conversations with Airl, and other DEF personnel, have begun to be filled in with light, form and life. Also, the understandings are substantial, accurate and will help to emancipate your from the false "reality" built upon the memories installed in your mind by the amnesia and mind-control operation of The Brothers of The Serpent!

Let us begin by describing the differences between your life on Earth, as a captive of and long-time resident of The Old Empire, and the universe of the IS-BEs who are from The Domain. You will discover that the contrast between these two "universes" will be very enlightening to you in your personal effort of "self-recovery".

The following Introductory Reorientation Material has been organized as a comparison between your life in the physical universe, on Earth, and your life in The Domain, and as a member of the DEF, using several general categories, as follow.

After you have reviewed each of these sections, your personalized rehabilitation program will begin:

## DIFFERENCES BETWEEN EARTH and THE DOMAIN

1. Physical Universe Survival vs.. The IS-BE
2. Physical Universe IS-BE Behavior vs. Domain IS-BE Behavior
3. Human Games vs. Domain Games
4. Physical Universe Time vs. Domain Time
5. Amnesia vs. Memory (of Identity, locations, activities and possessions)
6. Planetary Environments vs. IS-BE Universes
7. Body Hierarchy
8. Technology of Entrapment
9. Intentional Chaos vs.. Benevolent Control
10. Language vs.. Communication by Intention
11. The Tree of Life vs. Psionics
12. Sensation: Perception vs. Creation

### 1) Physical Universe Survival vs.. The IS-BE

Even though this unit of the DEF base is located in the asteroid belt (the shattered chunks of a planet that was blasted to bits in an ancient war) far away from the DEF Central Command Facility, we have access to The Domain Expeditionary Force Research Archives. These Archives include information from reconnaissance missions that complete their research far in advance, and as preparation for, the launch of an actual invasion force into new universes, galaxies or other spatial zones designed by The Domain for acquisition.

According the DEF Research Archive , the Physical Universe is only one many possible universes that coexist, independently, and exclusively of the others. Each universe, when it has grown to a size or magnitude worthy of consideration for invasion by The Domain, has been imagined, conjured and constructed by one, or more, IS-BEs.

In the case of the Physical Universe, this is a solidified amalgamation of the independent universes created by innumerable IS-BEs through a near infinity of time. For an Immortal Spiritual Beings, the idea of survival is the outcome of an extensive, convoluted and distorted series of ideas and events that have devolved through a nearly infinite period of time.

Before the beginning of the physical universe there had existed, for a nearly infinite duration, indefinable in terms of time, a concatenation of IS-BE whose ability to create an illusion were immense and incomprehensible in terms of time, space, objects or energy. The closest approximation would be to describe them as "magic".

Of course, magic is in the eye of the observer of inexplicable events or phenomenon. Let it suffice to say that the interplay of "magic", and counter-play of magicians, one against the others, resulted in a universe of phenomenon which are still dimly recalled by IS-BEs in the physical universe, who had once been a part of this earlier wizardry and wonder.

As the ability and power required of an IS-BE to act as a wizard or god, is largely forbidden, forgotten and forsaken in this universe by it's jealous inhabitants, there is little need to speculate on the nature of it beyond the observation that it no longer seems to exist as a "reality". Nonetheless, children and some few artists can still recall brief snatches of serenely splendid and / or tumultuously terrible events which are retold in fairy tales, comic books, fantasies and fables.

Originally, each IS-BE, or group of IS-BE created in a space and into which illusions were conjured. Just as you create any object in your mind, by imagination, it remains there only so long as you continue to imagine it. When you remove your creative attention, the object disappears. So to, were those universes.

Eventually, these IS-BEs grew tired of having to continually perpetuate an illusion in order to have a universe. Apparently, this laziness, so to speak, was spawned by the desire to have one's creative illusions admired by other IS-BEs.

So, in order to sustain an illusion long enough to be viewed and admired by others, IS-BEs began to make there illusions linger, by making them out of solid particles, rather than thought alone.

The concept of an "eternal" universe, that would endure forever, could be built of indestructible particles, consolidated into larger forms, could be used as building material in an ever-expanding space. The theory was sound, perhaps, but the actualization was flawed in that, once built, it could not be "unbuilt".

A small analogy is the painter who carefully places bits of colored pigment on a canvas so that their "universe" will remain in place long enough to be seen and admired by others.

The lust for admiration of ones own creation, so universally exhibited in the behavior of IS-BEs who created what came to be the physical universe, seems to be the lowest common denominator that ended in a coalescence of all IS-BE universes into one, combined universe made of everlasting bits of energy and matter.

Overly a nearly infinite time IS-BEs expanded the practice of perpetual creation of energy and objects to be admired until a creation, if not admired sufficiently, was abandoned, while the IS-BE went off to create other solid illusions which he hoped would attract more attention from others.

Eventually, this free-for-all of creation degenerated into a sort of "game", wherein the players competed for admiration. Illusions, in order to be perpetual, were subjected to alteration, or modification. Continued, ad infinitum, the "game" degenerated into increasingly more elaborate, convoluted tricks and charades of petty competitive jealousies, that enabled counter-creation, and destruction of the creations of others.

IS-BEs joined together in groups to make bigger, more complex and sustainable illusions. Other groups opposed them. Others stole or destroyed the creations of others. When one becomes a member of a larger group it is very difficult to maintain an individual identity. The IS-BEs forgot that they, individually, were the "god" or creator of universes.

Periodically, IS-BE from other universes invaded and conquered all or parts of the physical universe, just a The Domain is doing at this time. In so doing, the creative or destructive elements of those IS-BEs and their own universes were commingled to further complicate and confuse this universe. To date there have been six such incursions, the fifth and six of which are ongoing at this time.

Ultimately, the IS-BEs gave up their individual creative power, lost in the confusion of mutually created, altered, destroyed and abandoned ideas, illusions, energy and objects.

Galaxies of scattered, shattered planets, gaseous clouds, negative energies, radiant stars, swirling in an infinite vacuum of black space is the resulting residue of the contest for admiration between IS-BEs in this universe.

And what of the IS-BEs themselves? Who are the creators, conjurors, collaborators, who are, individually and collectively, the "god" of this universe? As far as The Domain has determined, they are the only surviving inhabitants of an ancient, post-apocalyptic "home" they built for themselves. A home that they built, remodeled, destroyed, and rebuilt from ruined rubble, and billion, billion, billion times over.

The history of Earth is a microcosmic reflection of the macrocosmic decay of the physical universe. And, as unpleasant as the reality of a prison planet may be, the image of the "Creator" can be seen reflected in the bathroom mirrors of Earth and every planet in the myriad galaxies.

Every creature who is a citizen of this IS-BE community is now captive within the crumbled walls of an unadmired citadel of their mutual creation.

The purpose of The Domain Expeditionary Forces, inspired by the principle of "All-Mother" in The Eternally Benevolent Domain, is to recover, not only our own IS-BEs who are captive on Earth, but any other IS-BE who may still be willing and able to recognize and rediscover the creative powers required to create, and co-create, universes with imagination.

There are other universes. The Domain in one such. It is a universe in which an IS-BE can play a game, free from the lust for admiration, which is the ultimate and inevitable folly that leads to the of destruction of all imagination and illusion.

***Essentially, the difference between The Eternally Benevolent Domain and the Physical Universe is this:***

**The maxim of the Physical Universe is SURVIVAL.**

Survival is accomplished by persisting in an established environment. The physical universe has already been created, the rules firmly set, the objects and spaces are solid and indestructible. Innovation is not permitted. Agreement is mandatory.

**The maxim of The Domain is BE and/or CREATE.**

To BE is the definition of an IS-BE. A state of being is sufficient unto itself as an activity, or non-activity, for an IS-BE. For the majority of IS-BEs creation is the fundamental state of being.

Being and creation are unlimited, indefinable qualities from which any universe is conjured. That a universe must be sustained and solidified in order to be a universe is not required. The instant of creation, repeated, causes persistence in a universe, and makes perception and communication within a universe possible between IS-BEs. However, a creation can be erased, or altered, simply by creating a new, or different creation. The Domain is a continual, cooperative act of creation between IS-BEs who are bound by the principle of All-Mother, under the guidance of Omnimat.

**WE CREATE THE ETERNALLY BENEVOLENT DOMAIN!**

## 2) Physical Universe IS-BE Behavior vs. Domain IS-BE Behavior

The principle and fundamental differences between IS-BEs of The Domain and the IS-BEs of the physical universe, are few and simple:

- Physical universe IS-BEs demand the playing of a game. They consider that they, themselves, do not or can not exist without an amusement provided to them by overcoming obstacles interposed to obstruct the attainment of some imagined goal, status, or possession.
- Each component part of a game is an artificial contrivance, which the players pretend to be "real".
- The players agree that space exists in which barriers and the goals are real, and desirable.
- IS-BEs create objects in the space with which to play.
- Once created, objects may not be destroyed, although they may be altered in form.
- The fundamental purpose of all games is having a game to play.
- Boredom is the undesirable state of being for which the playing of games is thought to be an elixir or remedy.
- A game is a condition that requires agreement, motion and admiration, or, that admiration be withheld from players.

- Gaining admiration from other players is the most desirable goal for any game.
- In the physical universe, it is forbidden NOT to participate in the game, even as a spectator.
- Every IS-BE is required, by agreement, to participate in the game, either as a proponent of a goal, an opponent of a goal, or as a spectator.
- Goals, or rules for playing, are created by relatively few IS-BEs but agreed upon by many, so that the number of players is maximized.
- The ultimate outcome of every such game in the physical universe is that all the players and bystanders are crushed into becoming "pawns" in a state of endless turmoil and chaos which gradually coalesces into a solidity that becomes the universe itself.
- No victory or escape in the game is possible. If there ever were to be a "victory", the game would end!
- The game is never allowed to end. It is eternal, and ever-expanding, just as the playing field upon which the game is played, the physical universe, expands eternally.
- The motions of the players and the playing field is monitored by the players. This is called time.

IS-BEs of The Domain have not such agreements, conditions or impositions placed upon them by other IS-BEs of The Domain.

Every IS-BE is allowed to coexist, freely. Of course games certainly do exist in The Domain. But, the IS-BEs who play in these games do so willingly, if they chose to participate at all.

The DEF is one such game in which all of the "players" or personnel in the game of voluntary participants. They can enter and leave to game at will without recrimination or expectation from the others. No admiration is required.

However, the degree of integrity associated with the promise or agreement given by an IS-BE to another IS-BE or group of IS-BEs within The Domain in inviolate. Once given, an IS-BE in The Domain does not relent until his or her agreement has been fulfilled.

**WE CREATE THE ETERNALLY BENEVOLENT DOMAIN!**

### 3) Games vs. All-Mother

The primary difference between IS-BEs of The Domain and those of the physical universe is the condition known as "games". In The Domain it has long been observed that in order for each individual IS-BE to remain free from intrusion or tyranny imposed on them by more powerful, or less ethical IS-BEs, we must cooperate to defend and nurture each other. A principle of benevolent mutual respect for all IS-BEs, and the universes they create / occupy, is referred to as "All-Mother".

"All-Mother" is a philosophy in which the behavior or conduct of an individual and groups of IS-BEs is adjudicated based on the logical premise that in order to sustain optimum freedom, order and serenity for all IS-BEs, each IS-BE must serve all IS-BEs.

This premise is not intended to eliminate disagreements between IS-BEs, but to mitigate destruction or chaotic behavior between them.

"All-Mother" assures the inherent right of an individual IS-BE to approach, depart from, or not interact, with other IS-BEs while maintaining an optimum serenity.

The purpose of The Domain is to defend the right of an individual or group of IS-BEs to create a universe, or not, at their own discretion.

It has been observed that when responsibility for maintaining organization within the co-created universe shared by all IS-BEs is not defended and preserved, each individual IS-BE is deprived of the freedom assured by the power of a collaborative, creative will and combined power.

***The Omniscient and Omnipotent Matriarch*** (abbrev: Omnimat) is an IS-BE who acts as magistrate of The Domain.

- Through preeminent power, wisdom and benevolence, Omnimat supervises and enforces the principle of All-Mother within The Domain.
- Omnimat does not create, destroy or alter universes.
- Omnimat may, or may not, enforce penalties or restrictions upon IS-BEs when violations of the principle of All-Mother occur within The Domain.
- The discretion and judgment of Omnimat are inviolate.
- Omnimat enforces all judgments.

To the degree that IS-BEs of The Domain do not need or desire admiration, and are not compelled to "play" a game at all times, the power, stability and serenity of The Domain remains relatively stable, when compared to the physical universe.

(The physical universe is, by definition, an infinite, icy void cluttered with random sources of savage energy combined with mindless chunks of matter. The massive and chaotic construction of the physical universe is utterly antipathetic to the spiritual "nothingness" which is the intelligent source of life forms and of universes.)

It is imperative that the essential freedom, serenity, social order and power of The Domain be preserved and disseminated across other universes. Thereby, the well-being of all IS-BEs is served.

### 4) Physical Universe Time vs. Domain Time

The concept of time in the physical universe is derived from an arbitrary measurement of the motion of objects through space. Although the space of the Physical Universe is nearly immeasurable, and continually expanding, the entire space and all of the objects in it are in the same time.

The frequency or cyclical pattern of the movement of objects in space, when measured, constitute a method of "time keeping". The measurement is modified by the point of view from which the space and objects are viewed.

The importance assigned to the objects and their motion, is relative to the point of view of the viewer. For example, "time" to a hummingbird is not the same as "time" for a sloth. Likewise, "time" for a space ship pilot traveling several trillion light-years in a day, is not the same as "time" for a human being on Earth, who must inhale one breath oxygen every few seconds in order to avoid body death within five minutes.

The frequency of this vibration is one of the many phenomena which define the peculiar characteristics of the physical universe. However, it must be carefully noted that these phenomenon are specific to the physical universe ONLY. They do not apply to any other universes encountered by The Domain Expeditionary Forces, so far.

By contrast, time in The Domain is not necessarily limited to the constraints defined by the laws or agreements of a single space or universe. Inasmuch as there are a nearly infinite number of universes, each with there own measurements of "time", or "state" of existence, or "no-time", The Domain, and DEF Personnel must operate within the relative rules or conventions for each universe respectively.

For example, in the physical universe, the DEF measures time in terms of "mission cycles". Each mission cycle has the equivalent value of 5,000 Earth Solar years. This is due to the observation that it is convenient for DEF missionaires to volunteer for duty for a period of not less than one mission cycle. Also, serving with the DEF for less than one mission cycle is not practical in that any significant mission objective and target requires significant logistics, coordination and execution.

In short, time is relative to the rules of each individual universe.

Universes can vary widely according to the creative ideas and opinions of each individual IS-BE. Each IS-BE is a universe unto themselves. An IS-BE can change their "mind" or opinion about anything and everything at the speed of thought. Therefore, a universe can exist in one moment of "time" and not exist in the next. Many universes may coexist simultaneous, either interacting or not, without reference to any others.

In the same fashion, groups of IS-BEs, through collaboration and agreement, can create, perpetual, alter and "un-create" universes, and therefore, time.

As a result of the sequential measurement of objects, (events) in the physical universe space, one can tack a sequential series of motions, such as the rotation of planets around a star, the movements of stars within galaxies, galaxies relative to other galaxies, and so forth. IS-BEs use this sequential time as a tool to judge the relative "age" of events in their own experience.

This is what IS-BEs in the physical universe call "memory". This memory is maintained and considered to be "sacred" by each IS-BE. These usually take the form of pictures, sensations, and motion recordings.

The memory is stored in the sequence in which the events or motions of the physical universe were observed, from his or her personal vantage point. IS-BEs often share or trade their memories with other IS-BEs as a convenient way to expand their own experiences.

Although this is a convenient tool for the IS-BE, it violates the essential spiritual state of the IS-BE, which is a continuous moment of "is" emanating from a decision or thought to "be". Therefore, there is no actual "time" for an IS-BE. However, when an IS-BE has forgotten this fundamental fact, for the sake of playing a game, this artificial "time" factor can prove to be a liability.

A secondary factor, in the specialized case of IS-BEs who have had "memory" erased and altered by the BOTS, is that one can not measure the passage of time using the "deteriorization of matter" as a clock to determine the "age" of objects.

The reason for this is that a fundamental building block of the physical universe is the "conservation of energy". That is to say that all energy, particles and objects are made of condensed particles in the physical universe. Each particle is indestructible. Each particle of energy or matter, no matter how gargantuan or miniscule, was created by the "thought" of an IS-BE.

This is why the physical universe in a "ever-expanding" universe. IS-BEs continue to create, combine, solidify, dissemble, recombine particles and objects in space, but the original particles always exist.

One can "destroy" a mountain or a star by dispersing them into their original particles, but the particles themselves cannot be destroyed. Although a mountain, or statue or ocean may dissolve, the component particles remain unaltered.

Many of the inmates on Earth were told that history written by priests that record the time track of hypnotic commands of the BOTS, gave the age of "creation" of the physical universe as 3987 B.C.E.

On Earth, the estimation of the age of the planet, and the universe, using the "deteriorization of matter" as a theoretical gauge, contributes greatly to perpetuate the amnesia / hypnosis mechanism on the BOTS prison planet. The most recent mythology being preached by the prison system priests, and scientists to the inmate population of Earth, is that the universe is only four and a half billions years old!

Of course, these absurd impossibilities are an excellent demonstration of how powerful and overwhelming the BOTS amnesia / hypnosis mechanism can be!

A routine hypnotic trick the BOTS use to reinforce amnesia is to reverse memory, or history. This mechanism creates the illusion that events that have already occurred in the past have not yet happened, but may be possible in the future, and visa versa.

On Earth, writers of science fiction commonly describe events that actually took place billions or trillions of years ago, but attribute these events to the future. In part, this is a reason that people describe "modern" architecture, or design as "futuristic". In fact, these designs have been remembered from ancient civilizations from which the artists or designers were captured and sent to Earth as "untouchables".

The memory of an IS-BE can never be permanently erased. However, it make be covered, like a curtain, with force, deception, and trickery. When the trickery is revealed, the curtain is lifted and accurate memories may be restored.

The actual "age" of Earth, and the physical universe cannot be determined precisely, but is certainly on the order of several quadrillion Earth years. This estimate is based on the first hand observations and records of IS-BE from The Domain, and from the physical universe, who, during their nearly infinite immortality, remember when a preceding universe decayed, and gradually devolved into the "solid" universe resulting from the "collision" of many universes.

Written and pictographic books, and military records captured from the Old Empire central government planet in the Draco system, recently destroyed by the DEF (8,050 B.C.E.), indicate a similar age.

**WE CREATE THE ETERNALLY BENEVOLENT DOMAIN!**

**5) Amnesia vs. Memory**

The Brothers of The Serpent have used the phenomenon of "time" and "conservation of energy" to create mental "tricks" or delusions, which when combined with overwhelming force of electronic weapons, can cause an IS-BE to "forget" everything they have observed or experienced in the physical universe.

This tremendous electronic force, when focused intensely on the IS-BE, and combined with a hypnotic command to "forget" causes a loss of memory or amnesia. When the force is magnified, and, at the same instant, a "false memory" is forced onto the IS-BE, this can cause "permanent" memory loss.

The IS-BE memory is not actually lost, but the IS-BE conceives that it is "gone" because the electronic force, combined with the hypnotic suggestion, acts like a magicians "slight of hand", to misdirect the attention of the IS-BE long enough to "erase and replace" the actual memory.

An additional "trick" the DEF Mission discovered recently is the BOTS shock / hypnosis mechanism can be used to superimpose a "reverse" time track on the IS-BE. This is commonly seen in science fiction books and motion pictures on Earth, wherein experiences or memories of the "past" are reversed and called "futuristic". An IS-BE can become quite confused and disoriented by these tricks.

These are the fundamental mechanisms, used repeatedly (after the death and departure from a body by an IS-BE at the end of each lifetime) by the BOTS to create and maintain a "prison" on Earth. All of the "prisoners" are "treated" in this fashion. This is why it is essential that the mechanisms of the BOTS, which are installed throughout this end of the galaxy, be discovered and destroyed for the DEF.

Fortunately, an IS-BE does not truly, ever, forget who they are, but their memory can be submerged by electronic forces that make the IS-BE very reluctant to "remember". Or, the memory can be supplanted by "false memories" or hypnotic suggestions that create the delusion that the past is the future, and so forth.

The DEF is working on enhancing our ability to reverse the adverse effects of the BOTS operation. However, this has proven to be a tedious, one-on-one procedure, as you, yourself are experiencing.

We have learned to drastically accelerate memory recovery by exposing the IS-BE to images or pictures of actual objects, events, places, and events that are familiar to the IS-BEs own, personal experiences. However, these experiences differ from one IS-BE to the next.

In the case of DEF personnel, such as yourself, we have the advantage of transporting you, as an IS-BE, back to a Domain Central Base, from which your entire personal "history" can be reconstructed from The Domain Archives. When you are exposed to enough of the experiences, places, friendships, languages and familiar "possessions" of your life in The Domain, you will naturally "remember" your actual identity.

Unfortunately, the DEF in unable to use this convenient short-cut for the rest of the IS-BEs on Earth, as they are still inhabiting a biological body, and cannot be transported anywhere in a space craft. Nor would such an undertaking be practical, even if it were possible, as biological bodies are far, far too fragile to endure the rigors of intergalactic space, much less the tremendous logistics involved in keeping a biological body alive in a sustainable planetary civilization!

The "home" planets of these IS-BEs may still exist, but the Old Empire influences that made them "untouchable" are still in place. It is unlikely that this condition of cultural and spiritual tyranny will be changed in this galaxy in the foreseeable future.

Although The Domain is willing to assist, we do not have authorization of invest resources in salvaging the general population of Earth at this time. According the current Domain Invasion Schedule it will be only one mission cycle before the main body of our invasion force reaches this galaxy, at which time other uses have been designated for Earth.

Until that time, the IS-BE "inmates" of Earth are left to recover their own memory, and, if possible, get themselves out of prison. If they are unable to do so, we are unable to assist them, as there are higher priorities, as designated by DEF Command Authority.

**WE CREATE THE ETERNALLY BENEVOLENT DOMAIN!**

## 6) Planetary Environments vs. IS-BE Universes

Earth is identified by The Domain as a Class 7 planet, heavy gravity, nitrogen/oxygen atmosphere planet, with biological life-forms, in proximity to a single, yellow, medium-size, low-radiation, type 12 star". (The proper designations are difficult to translate accurately due to the extreme limited astronomical nomenclature of the North American English language.)

Earth is unusual in that the majority of the land-masses are covered with water. It could be just as easily be classified as a Class 9 Planet (liquid surface), if the liquid were more desirable as a resource to be harvested for use in The Domain. Since DEF personnel do not inhabit biological bodies water is undesirable in space.

In addition, Earth is extraordinary in that it is virtually uninhabitable by any sustainable civilization for more than a very short period. It has a superheated, liquefied metal core, on top of which the land masses drift and crash into each other causing volcanic eruptions that poison the atmosphere. Virtually constant earthquake activity devastate the land. Also, the magnetic poles, generated by the molten core, shift every 20,000 years or so, which displaces the oceans randomly, overwhelming land masses with devastating deluges.

Human beings, is a species of life inhabited by the "untouchable" IS-BEs from around this, and adjoining galaxies. Humankind was placed on Earth a little more than 100,000 years ago. Little of value is known about the history of Earth except that it is not considered to be a very useful resource by The Domain. The moon of Earth, the planet Venus, and especially the asteroid belt are useful bases for low-gravity landings, and serve as a good "rest stop" along the invasion course toward the center of this galaxy and beyond.

Planets can serve as habitats for IS-BE inhabiting a nearly infinite variety of life-forms. Each planetary environment serves as host for species of life that have been engineered to utilize the natural resources of the planet. In The Domain, IS-BEs do not need or use bodies to operate or perceive or move or play games, or communicate.

Although The Domain pervades and operates across a vast region of physical universe space, it is not a civilization inhabited by IS-BEs who created this universe. The Domain pervades many other universes.

The origin universe of The Domain is one that is a mutually created and sustained "illusion". It does not exist in solid, physical form. Rather, it is a body of thought energy, co-created by the combined imaginations and communication of spiritual entities.

The unifying force that binds the beings of The Domain into a singular identity, or civilization, is the concept of "All-Mother". Omnimat is both an omniscient, omnipresent, omnipotent spiritual being, who serve as the benevolent guardian of the philosophical principle that is embodied in the principle of All-Mother.

This concept is expressed simply and precisely in the **Doctrine of The Eternally Benevolent Domain:**

*"The Goal of The Eternally Benevolent Domain is to unite all immortal spiritual beings, space, energy and possessions to form a vast, multi-dimensional civilization guided by the transcendent principle of All-Mother, under the supervision of The Omniscient and Omnipotent Matriarch."*

The physical universe was not created, monitored or guided by a single, benevolent IS-BE. Rather, it is a the coalescence, amalgamation and solidification of interacting, conflicting and chaotic IS-BEs and groups of IS-BEs. The common denominators of the physical universe are objects in space manipulated by forces of energy exerted against them.

IS-BEs who create, and organize energy and matter into orderly forms are in continual conflict with those who prefer destruction and chaos. The entire universe is the residue of perpetual creation, organization, alteration and destruction by various energy forces exerted by IS-BE against each other.

**WE CREATE THE ETERNALLY BENEVOLENT DOMAIN!**

## 7) IS-BE vs. Body

The IS-BEs of The Domain permeate every conceivable dimension, space, universe, zone, or environment. A spiritual being can "be" any form, and / or no form, at will. An IS-BE, as the spiritual, non-physical entity, creates it's own energy, but has no physical characteristics, or location in space or time.

An IS-BE can move in, around and through objects and spaces as thought alone. They communicate and perceive thought directly between themselves.

Obviously, an IS-BE who is capable of creating illusions and emitting energy can "send" telepathic communication more effectively than those who are less able to do so. For this reason, Officers in the DEF are the more powerful and effective "senders" of thought. A far greater number of beings can perceive or receive thoughts than those who are able to project them.

There exists a social, economic, political and cultural hierarchy or class system throughout the planets of the Old Empire, as well as most of the remaining physical universe, so far as the DEF has been able to detect. This hierarchy is based on an arbitrary designation of body types as "desirable" or not.

Of course, as with any political or economically based organization, this structure or "order", is decided upon and enforced by the "highest" class, the most powerful, and, usually, the most oppressive.

This class hierarchy is formed by assigning each IS-BE to inhabit a certain type of body. When an IS-BE loses the power to control or defend their own space, illusions, thoughts and self-orientation, he or she becomes the victim of others who prefer to control other IS-BEs to serve them. Control, when applied for the purpose of personal gain, and to the detriment of others, results in oppression and slavery.

Slavery, for IS-BEs, is the most common and pervasive state of existence across the black, barren vacuums of never-ending space, amid swirling balls of cold, lifeless matter. Some of these are sporadically illuminated by spheres of relentless radioactive fire.

This slavery, for biological life forms, is ensured by bondage to the idea of "survival". For an IS-BE, survival is a laughable and contemptible absurdity! How can an immortal spiritual essence of infinite power and ability NOT persist?

As with all hucksters, shysters, charlatans and slave masters, the "problem" of immortality was solved with lies, deceit, trickery, propaganda and vicious brutality. By degrees, IS-BEs we sold, indoctrinated, coerced and forced into "believing" that they must have an external source of energy in order to exist. This chicanery is made complete when <u>some</u> of the IS-BEs become the slave masters, simply by controlling the alleged energy sources.

This supposed "energy" began as "admiration": something for which all IS-BEs in the physical universe with insatiably hungry.

Progressively, the energy became more and more solid, as did the universe, and as were the "slave bodies" that were employed to build it. Eventually, solid bodies were engineered and constructed to perform specific tasks, using various forms of energy to motivate, reward or "feed" them.

The most frequently used forms of energy are light, radiation, electricity, vapors, aesthetics, intoxicants, and sexual sensation. The perception of various aesthetic sensations, such as sex, aroma, taste, texture, pressure, heat and cold, are installed into the human bodies with a combination of aesthetics and pain which may become as addictive to the IS-BE as any habit-forming drug.

Biological body sensations include the two of the most decadent of all:

Sex, which is a specialized perception that combines the opposite of exquisite aesthetics with painful electrical shock. And, hunger, excited by the odor, texture and flavor of "food" made of dead organic life forms!

Once the IS-BE is "addicted" to the energy form, it is a simple matter to withhold, or create an artificial scarcity of the energy, to keep the slaves running on an absurd economic treadmill like a donkey chasing a carrot on a stick.

The long and dismal trail of deception and degradation culminated in the existing IS-BE social and economic hierarchy, which is organized approximately, as follows:

- IS-BEs who are Independent from bodies
- IS-BEs who have limited a dependence on bodies

(there are many gradients of this "class", defined by a political / economic scale of relative freedom and responsibility to the society, government or organization of which they are members)

- IS-BE who use mechanical bodies or "doll bodies"

(these are usually assigned to very capable beings who are able to enter into and exit from a material object at will. Such beings and bodies are used to perform specific industrial or military functions. The complexity and variety of these are highly specialized according to the demands of the tasks to be performed.)

- IS-BEs who are no longer able to depart from a solid object once they have entered into it.

(these beings are assigned -- and forced -- to inhabit a nearly infinite range of body types specifically designed for each Class of Planet or physical environment, or function to be performed.)

- IS-BEs who inhabit only organic, biodegradable bodies

(these vary widely according to planetary environments)

- IS-BEs who have been declared "untouchable".

(these are the IS-BEs who have been expelled from various civilizations because they can not be coerced or enticed to conform with the social / economic / political / military infrastructure. This includes all of the beings on Earth.)

Within this hierarchy, the biological body is the least desirable and most despised of any IS-BE civilization, for obvious reasons. The biological body is easiest to control and destroy because of its incomparable fragility, utter dependence on external energy sources, and sensitivity to sensation and pain.

Any self-respecting, independent IS-BE would never knowingly allow themselves to inhabit a frail, flimsy, inflexible, piece of flesh. This is why the BOTS, and other civilizations, have resorted to the use of such extraordinary, overwhelming electronic force, deception, trickery and continual covert coercion. An IS-BE must be degraded into an unthinkably disabled state to be trapped and held captive against their will in a biological body!

In The Domain, biological bodies are not used. If any body is used at all, it is only in cases where the DEF is operating in the physical universe. And then, only as authorized by specific Mission Orders, such a those assigned in the current DEF Invasion Schedule.

Of course, any Independent IS-BE can occupy any body they want to -- at their own risk. But, not even DEF Officers are ever required to do so as part of their official duties in the DEF. The risks, observed over a very long period, have proven to be far too great. Once an IS-BE has entered into a body, and for whatever reason, is unable to get OUT again, the IS-BE can not be extracted. There is no known method to do so.

This is part of the reason that the DEF Rescue and Recovery mission has experienced such great difficulty in recovering the 3,000 members of the lost battalion. We are truly exploring unknown territory when dealing with bodies -- most especially biological bodies.

Apparently, biological bodies were originally engineered to serve as "amusements" for IS-BEs, such as the creatures that were created to populate zoological garden planets. It was never conceived that an Independent IS-BE would "become" a body.

However, within the seemingly inevitable "games" of the physical universe, anything and everything is eventually used as a weapon of destruction or a method of making slaves of other IS-BEs. This is certainly the case with bodies. No better prison cell or set of chains was every invented with which to capture, control, and coerce an IS-BE into submission!

The BOTS have complicated this mess and confusion with hypnotically implanted false "emotions", sexual compulsions, bizarre mythology, dramatic social fantasies, and outright lies designed to distract the attention of the IS-BE from realizing the simple serenity and power that is the natural condition of the IS-BE.

**WE CREATE THE ETERNALLY BENEVOLENT DOMAIN!**

## 8) Technology of Entrapment

Since the destruction of the BOTS space fleet in the Earth solar system in1230 AD, some of the oppressive thought control activity against IS-BEs on Earth was reduced, resulting in a resurgence of technology. A human population had existed for thousands of years without the most rudimentary technologies of civilization, many of which are dependent on the use of electricity.

After the destruction of the BOTS base in the Cydonia region of Mars, and the "seeding" of certain technical knowledge by Officer Airl during her visit with you in 1947, a quantum leap in technical advancements have resulted on Earth. Many of these advancements are related to the use of integrated computer circuits, and to a lesser degree, fiber optic cable.

Consequently, in less than 100 years, IS-BEs on Earth have had their "memory" partially rekindled regarding how to create and use hundreds of technologies they already knew from civilizations of the planets from which they were brought to Earth.

Just a suddenly as the "false facade" pyramid civilizations were set up by the BOTS on Earth 6,000 years earlier, the partial disruption of the BOTS mind-control operation has released barriers that have prevented the IS-BEs of Earth from remembering billions of years of technical development.

However, the BOTS mind-control mechanisms are still very heavily entrenched around Earth, and the prison planet operation is still active. The inability of the DEF to fully detect and destroy this operation has frustrated our efforts to rescue our own personnel who remain trapped in that maze of duress and deceit.

This is all the more astonishing to the members of the DEF rescue mission in that our own extremely sophisticated technology, combined with our ability to operate as Independent IS-BEs, is unparalleled by any known civilization in the physical universe.

The "Tree of Life" developed by the DEF missionaires proved to be very effective tool for detecting the presence and identity of an IS-BE. The device is used to detect and measure the IS-BE "signature" of those members of the Lost Battalion who are still on Earth. This "signature", which is unique to each individual, is the field of energy produced by every IS-BE outside a body, and is the energy that animates the body when inhabited by an IS-BE. These qualities of this energy can be sensed visually as an aura, and experienced by other IS-BEs as emotion.

By tracing these "signatures" we have been able to determine that the signature "disappears" in certain areas of space on or around Earth. Conversely, a short time after the IS-BE signature disappears, the IS-BE often reappears again back on Earth -- inside a biological body!

This is how DEF missionaires we able to discover the locations of AQERTs in the Pyrenees Mountains, in the Rwanda

Mountains of Africa, as well as in the steppes of Mongolia, on Mars, and several areas at this end of the Milky Way galaxy.

After several hundred cases of this phenomenon were detected, it became apparent that this is a repeating cycle for all of the IS-BEs on Earth. It became equally obvious that the BOTS use methods of control over IS-BEs that enforce this behavior. The exact methods of this control are not fully understood, but many of the fundamental principles have been observed in the "footprints" left by the behavior of IS-BEs on Earth.

Since the destruction of the BOTS space fleet and the Mars installation, the BOTS operation has gone completely underground. Their entire mind-control operation is extremely well hidden and protected by impenetrable force fields.

However, the DEF has accumulated a lot of information about the BOTS by observing their "footprints". Our rescue mission on Earth has been very much like tracking a giant alien beast through a tropical jungle, where footprints and traces are continually washed away by torrential rains. We find an occasional footprint, or broken tree branch, a tuft of hair, a scent or fecal dropping, but we have not yet seen or captured a living specimen. We know they exist, but we have yet to see one.

By the observing the phenomenon surrounding the location of AQERTs, we know that these operate like an electronic "tractor screen" or an IS-BE "spider web" in space. Rather than emanating a field of force, the force field is used to "pull in" the

IS-BE. These fields are usually "baited" with some sort of enticement, such a images of beautiful buildings, or music.

The electronic technology used by the BOTS exhibits billions, if not trillions, of years of refinement. In addition, the installation of the electronic force screens, and underground bases on Earth, on Mars and throughout an entire sector of this galaxy they use to detect and capture IS-BEs demonstrates an extensive covert operation which must have taken millions of years to deploy.

In short, it appears that there is no quick, easy remedy for the condition of IS-BEs on Earth at this time. Unfortunately, all of the very formidable resources and technologies of The Domain have not been brought to bear to solve this problem. Therefore, it is unlikely that The Domain Expeditionary Force Central Command will authorize any additional resource to be deployed here for a least one more Mission Cycle, if at all.

There is no doubt that if a larger, more fully equipped mission were sent from The Domain to handle to matter, founded as we are in a trillion years of technology and accumulated wisdoms, and guided by Omnimat, the DEF could dissolve the prison planet mechanisms, destroy the BOTS installations and return deserving IS-BEs to their previous states of independence.

It must be clearly understood that technology alone is not effective unless it is applied by technicians who are guided by the principle of "All-Mother". A solution to this problem is only as efficacious as it nurtures the well-being of an IS-BE.

The perversion of technology on Earth by the BOTS mind-control operators, who control the priests of "science", as well a religion, is exemplified in atomic fission, which is a very crude and impractical energy resource, at best. These priests uniformly and universally apply "technology" for murderous military purposes because this serves the purposes of the BOTS: to keep the inmates of the Earth prison in a perpetual state of chaos and self-destruction.

For this reason, "technology" alone, will not be enough to solve the Earth prison situation. Humanitarian control, in the hands of IS-BEs on Earth who are natively aware of "All-Mother", must supplant and supersede the criminals who control the governments and resources of Earth.

Justifiably, a prison is necessary to isolate and prevent the small minority of criminals and maniacs in the universe from destroying the players and playing field. Just as one quarantines a diseased patient to prevent an epidemic, so must the destructive, criminally insane be quarantined from the majority of the population who are IS-BEs whose only intention is to play the game according to agreed upon rules.

DEF missionaires have come to the conclusion that in order for IS-BE independence to be restored on Earth, for the time being, it will have to be done by the prisoners themselves, from the inside. Obviously, a prison break of this epic magnitude will require a great deal of communication, cooperation and willingness to fight back against the oppression of the BOTS.

Before that can be done, the majority of IS-BEs on Earth must discover and enforce an orderly method to prevent the viciously insane, perverse and maniacal IS-BEs on Earth from destroying the rest.

The irretrievably insane, and destructive IS-BE population comprises about 20% of the total inmate population. These vary from stupid and disabled to the most clever and powerful, as witnessed in the repeated destruction of every civilization on Earth by economic chaos and war.

The criminally insane can be detected solely by their <u>actions</u>, whether these are overt or covert. Their evil <u>actions</u> define their actual intention to do harm. Rhetoric, propaganda, and promises are as empty and deadly to humanity as the frigid vacuum of space. IS-BEs of good will have been universally inept at facing this simply truth. Therefore, evil persists because we do not punish the <u>actions</u> of the criminally insane.

The politician, the banker, and the priest, are guided by the BOTS to form a Triangle of Entrapment on Earth. This is a simple, painless observation, easily made from the comfortable bases The Domain Expeditionary Force. We, who are not subject to enslavement inside pain-filled biological bodies, can perceive it, and are not effected.

However, on Earth, it must be observed with great caution that the procedures used to identify and quarantine these criminals is not administered by the criminals themselves. The operation of the prison system on Earth by The Brotherhood of The

Serpent is the result of the failure of a vast and ancient civilization of the "Old Empire" to administer justice with honesty and integrity.

The Domain, which is administered under the guidance of Omnimat, and the principle of "All-Mother", is the only known civilization in any universe we have yet encountered to have successfully mastered the subject of justice.

**WE CREATE THE ETERNALLY BENEVOLENT DOMAIN !**

## 9) Intentional Chaos vs. Benevolent Control

Apparently, chaos a the "natural" or "normal" state of existence in the physical universe. However, it must be observed that random, chaotic motion of objects, masses or energy in space is not accidental. Nothing is caused on any universe that has been created by the imaginative volition of IS-BEs which is not done as an intentional, premeditated action.

By contrast, in The Domain, the normal state is order, controlled under the guidance of Omnimat, based on the principle of "All-Mother". Chaos is antipathetic to an IS-BE in The Domain. By contrast, the IS-BEs of the physical universe, addicted as they are to the playing of games, do not tolerate order very well.

Although their are individual exceptions to the rule, they are not comfortable existing in a state of "being" without action or random motion, without which they become impatient and "bored".

Boredom is a symptom that one has lost the ability to create and sustain a self-created illusion, or universe. This disability eventually deteriorates in to such a low state of power for the IS-BE that the IS-BE can be tricked, overwhelmed, captured and enslaved by others. The prison planet system of Earth is an extreme example of this phenomenon.

Of course, this state could never exist in The Domain where Independent IS-BEs control and cooperate a universe so long as it is guided by Omnimat and the principle of "All-Mother".

The principle of "All-Mother" defines the agreed upon order of The Domain. The strength and pervasive awareness of Omnimat further ensures that all IS-BEs assist each other to maintain this order.

During the past 3,400 years on Earth, humans have been entirely at peace for only 268 of them, or just 8 percent of recorded history! (That is, a year in which fewer than 1,000 people were murdered in warfare.) The prison planet system of Earth is a supreme example of intentionally created chaos, where warfare, murder, theft, rape, and aggressive destruction are thought to be "normal", or even desirable.

At least 108 million people were killed in wars in the twentieth century. Estimates for the total number killed in wars throughout all of human history range from 150 million to 1 billion. Between 1900 AD and 1990 AD, 43 million soldiers died in wars. During the same period, 62 million civilians were killed. More than 34 million civilians died in World War II alone.

This wholesale slaughter and devastation our a part of the "intentional chaos" fomented by the mind-control / amnesia operation of the Brothers of The Serpent. It is based on the simple logic that, if the inmates are constantly destroying their civilizations and each other, they will never have an open, honest communication with each other. Without this communication, the realization that all of the IS-BEs of Earth are confined together in the same prison will never happen!

Warfare, instilled into "thoughts" of the "untouchable" madmen, who were deported from planetary systems throughout the Old Empire to Earth, are used to "inspire" millions of mindless IS-BEs, whose memories have been erased and replaced with false memories. The false memories contain heavy emotional command to "obey" their "leaders". The soldiers and citizens of each warring faction or nation are mentally implanted with an obedience called "faith", based on an convoluted moral code:

"We" are "right" and "they" are "wrong". Or, "We" are the "Chosen Ones" and everyone else is our "Enemy". Obviously, these ideas could only be conceived in the minds of psychotic, paranoid, murderers and thieves. In fact, these are the characteristics and moral code of The Brothers of The Serpent.

**WE CREATE THE ETERNALLY BENEVOLENT DOMAIN!**

## 10) Language vs. IS-BE Communication

Language, whether written or verbal, is based on a system of physical universe symbols. Each symbol is designed to represent a "thought". However, any symbol, or combination of symbols, as with a music score, mathematical equation, chemical formula, poem, or technical treatise, can only vaguely approximate the depth, breadth, subtle dimensions, textures, sensations, and a thousand diverse perceptions of a single thought when communicated directly between IS-BEs.

Throughout the nearly infinite existence of IS-BEs, direct thought communication has been universal. Not only is direct thought communication between IS-BEs the most accurate and comprehensive, it is also the easiest and most instantaneous. Thought is not located in space or time. It is conceived and projected by an IS-BE with the intention that it should be received and understood exactly as projected by the recipient.

Such communication enables the IS-BE who receives, or perceives it, to occupy the same point of view of the IS-BE who projected it. By comparison symbols or language, demand a multitude of alteration and condensation into physical universe masses and space.

The action of "translating" an IS-BE thought into symbols alters the communication so thoroughly that only a shadow of the original communication is can be received.

As a member of The Domain Expeditionary Force, especially those Independent IS-BEs who serve voluntarily as an officer, pilot, engineer, and mission personnel in open space, must be very excellent "senders" of communication "telepathically", to use the simplified Earth concept.

The ability and power of an IS-BE to "send" a communication is far greater than that required to be a "receiver". A simple analogy is the difference between a television network of broadcast towers or satellites that transmit information or programs, compared to a single television receiver.

IS-BEs of The Domain, especially DEF officers, are very powerful communications broadcasters. You will discover that your ability to send and receive communication directly with other IS-BEs will grow in strength and clarity as you exercise your inherent abilities to do so. Like a muscle, it gains strength with exercise, and skill with practice.

In DEF installations communication between DEF personnel is by direct thought. Translations and transmissions, such as the Reorientation Briefing you are currently studying, are used only when exact physical universe coordinates or technical information must be transmitted across physical universe space, such as between Galaxy 3793, Sun 12, Space Station 33 and our closest DEF Central Command Relay Outpost in Galaxy 263.

## 11) The Tree of Life vs. Psionics

As mentioned to you by Airl in the interviews you conducted with her in 1947 at Roswell US Air Force Base, The Domain missionaries developed and deployed an electronic "screening" device the help them detect and locate the IS-BEs of the DEF Missing Battalion on Earth.

The following is an excerpt from the transcripts of your interview with Airl on the subject:

*" The Domain Search Party devised a wide variety of electronic detection devices needed to track the electronic signature or wavelength of each of the missing members of the Battalion. Some were used in space, others on land, and special devices were invented to detect IS-BEs under water.*

*One of these electronic detection devices is referred to as a "tree of life". The device is literally a tool designed to detect the presence of life, which is an IS-BE. This was a large electronic screen generator designed to permeate wide areas. To the ancient humans on Earth it resembled a sort of tree, since is consists of an interwoven lattice of electronic field generators and receivers. The electronic field detects the presence of IS-BEs, whether the IS-BE is occupying a body, or if they are outside a body.*

*A portable version of this detection device was carried by each of the members of The Domain Search Party. Stone carvings in Sumeria show winged beings using pinecone-shaped instruments to scan the bodies of human beings. They are also shown carrying the power unit for the scanner which are depicted as stylized baskets or water buckets, being carried by eagle-headed, winged beings.*

*Members of the aerial unit of The Domain Search Party, led by Ahura Mazda, were often called "winged gods" in human interpretations. Throughout the Persian civilization there are a great many stone relief carvings that depict winged space craft, that they called a "faravahar"."*

The use of this electronic screening device, which was referred to by the ancient Assyrians, or Mesopotamians, as the "Tree of Life", proved to be a highly successful tool. The device emits a simple, low voltage, electronic force field. When the field contacts the force field emitted by an IS-BE, the device registers the exact "signature", or combination of energy characteristics, which uniquely identify every individual IS-BE.

However, such devices are limited for use with IS-BEs who are inside a body only. The DEF "Tree of Life" device is highly sensitive, and can detect and differentiate an IS-BE in space, under the ocean, inside of solid matter, and across great distances. It is not used as a therapeutic device.

Each IS-BE is a source of energy, with greater or lesser degrees of intensity or volume, depending on the inherent power of the IS-BE. This energy is the same energy, combined with thought, used by each IS-BE to animate matter, such as the bodies of various life forms.

One can observe this in a phenomenon variously called, on Earth, "electrography", and "corona discharge" that was investigated by scientists, including the DEF Officer, in human form, as Nikola Tesla, and various other individuals who introduced the technology to humans in the later 19th and early 20th centuries.

The DEF missionaires encountered various difficulties in detecting and communicating with IS-BEs on Earth. The principle difficulty is that an IS-BE, when trapped inside a biological body, has a limited ability to communicate with other IS-BEs. The very dense physical "screen" created by cells, chemicals, bone matter, nervous system of the body make it very difficult for the IS-BE to perceive and be perceived as a spiritual entity.

The necessity of using devices such as the Tree of Life became obvious in the early stages of the mission. Increasingly, it became apparent that electronic devices of greater sensitivity must be developed to penetrate this "body barrier", to assist in detecting subtle thoughts, emotions and energy emissions of the IS-BE while inside the body.

Your interviews with Officer Airl in 1947 were secretly distributed by the military to designated individual scientists, as well as military contractors and civilians. The number of persons who were vicariously exposed to or came into the possession of the transcripts is unknown. However, it is very obvious that certain technologies were "discovered" on Earth as a direct result of the visit of Officer Airl, which are numerous and widely varied in nature.

One of these "discoveries" was the "Hieronymous machine", which was patented in 1949 by Thomas G. Hieronymous, at that time a resident of Kansas City, Mo.. The machine was tested with positive results by the science fiction writer, and editor of *Astounding Science Magazine*, John W. Campbell. The machine was designed by the inventor to analyze the phenomenon of "eloptic radiation".

There are two basic types of these devices: Receivers and Transmitters. The Hieronymus machine is a Receiver instrument. It amplifies and detects the presence of "eloptic rays" which occur at different vibrational frequencies that occur naturally in all physical elements, like channel signals on a radio. These "rays" are inherent in all physical universe objects because the physical universe itself is created and sustained by IS-BE energy.

A refinement of the device called the electroencephaloneuromentimograph was devised by a chiropractor and author, Volney Mathison, who became active in psychoanalytical and biofeedback research after the interviews with Airl in 1947. His invention was attributed to his study of Carl Jung's theories of human psychology, to create a special lie-detector for examining unconscious and subconscious memories.

Control and diminution of the power of IS-BEs has been the principal activity of societies for trillions of years. War between IS-BEs, and war between IS-BEs and planetary civilizations, has been constantly recurrent in the physical universe from the very earliest moments of creating. The impulse of IS-BEs in the physical universe to be the "only one" and to destroy all the creations of others is the lowest common denominator of decay, solidification and death of societies.

The utter brutality and disregard for IS-BEs throughout the vast spaces -- about a quarter of the universe -- controlled by the Old Empire is too cruel to be imagined or remembered by anyone on Earth. The natural impulses of the majority of IS-BEs toward compassion, justice and equality are unknown qualities in the Old Empire. For this reason, the impulse of IS-BEs toward egalitarian societies, whether democratic or socialistic, persists as a revolutionary attempt to combat repression.

Only The Domain, under the guidance of Omnimat, can sustain an egalitarian association of IS-BEs.

**WE CREATE THE ETERNALLY BENEVOLENT DOMAIN!**

Traditional therapies described in the Vedas, as well as those taught by Guatama Siddhartha, and Loa-Tzu provided varying degrees of success until about 100 BCE, but were inevitably perverted and suppressed by priests, and other BOTS operatives.

Nearly 2,000 years later these techniques were able to be refined after the introduction of electric power to Earth by an independent DEF missionaire, Nicola Tesla. Without the broad availability of electricity on Earth, the use of sensitive electronic devices for therapeutic purposes was impossible.

A well trained and persistent physician can heal a patient with relative ease. However, a patient cannot be trained to heal themselves unless they become a physician. Training physicians is a long and arduous path, suitable to only a few extraordinary individuals.

After their departure from Earth, the infiltration of BOTS agents and priests routinely subvert the organizations that were established to administer the therapies to IS-BEs on Earth. The existence of escape routes from the prison planet are strictly and ruthlessly forbidden by the BOTS.

For this reason, as mentioned earlier, it has been determined that, for the moment, no further efforts will be made by the DEF to continue rescue efforts on Earth.

Of course, a few mystics, psychics, or spiritualists on Earth, have the ability to perceive an IS-BE, and communicate telepathically with them. This communication is the same whether the IS-BE is inside a body or outside. However the energy field and the perceptive abilities of an IS-BE, such as those on Earth, who have been given amnesia and forced into the crude confines of a biological body, are very limited indeed.

One of the hallmarks of an IS-BE who does not have amnesia, is that they have retained the ability to send and receive communication directly, which is a characteristic shared by all of officers and personnel of The Domain Expeditionary Force.

Although the Tree of Life has been used successfully to locate and identify many of the 3,000 members of the lost battalion, the DEF has not yet devised consistent and reliable methods to disable the AQERTs and other amnesia mechanisms of the Brothers of The Serpent. These mechanisms are powerful and pervasive, and made all the more effective by the thorough infusion of deceit, lies and trickery.

The religious organizations of Buddha and Tao "isms" that sprang up after the departure of the missionaires quickly destroyed the original philosophy and practice of the therapy they offered. Philosophical principles and practical therapies created to recover memory and ability of an IS-BE to escape from a flesh body, and from Earth, were replaced by ornate temples, priests, idol worship, rituals, chants, incantations and aesthetic ceremonies.

In their places, the prison planet priesthoods used the fundamental truths of these philosophies to establish highly profitable enticement for extortion operations, demanding money and subservience to the priesthood, in place of personal wisdom, responsibility and freedom.

It is an observable fact that once enslaved, many IS-BEs prefer to continue being slaves, voluntarily, rather than to face their personal responsibility for failing to oppose the IS-BEs who enslaved them, or for having helped to enslave their fellow IS-BEs.

This behavior is depended upon by the BOTS as a guarantee of their continuing ability to remain in power. As a final assurance, the entire planet of Earth, and the adjoining space of Galaxy 3793, is permeated with BOTS devices, which are virtually undetectable, and indestructible.

Were it not for the fact that these mechanisms capture and reinforce amnesia in the IS-BE every time the IS-BE departs from a body, the DEF mission might have been able to rescued all of the 3,000 members of the lost battalion thousands of years ago!

What remains, if one chooses to study and investigate carefully, are the philosophies and therapies developed by DEF missionaires which have successful enable some IS-BEs to escape. These must be studied and practiced in their original, unaltered forms. When altered, modified or "improved" by human "priests", these do not produce effective results.

Freedom and ability of every IS-BE, as embodied in the Principle of All-Mother, is an exemplary state of being.

**WE CREATE THE ETERNALLY BENEVOLENT DOMAIN!**

### 12) Sensation: Perception vs. Creation

During your interviews with Officer, Pilot and Engineer Airl, you were instructed on the fundamental construction and use of various body types.

During those interview, Airl did not provide information to you concerning the fundamental mechanism that attract IS-BEs into the physical universe, and ultimately trap them in it. This mechanism is based on the desire by the IS-BE to create a sensation effect on other IS-BEs, and to experience sensation. Any sensation can be conjured by an IS-BE. These are emitted, projected or perceived through the use of thought or as various forms of energy.

Both the projection and perception of sensation between IS-BEs can be an amusing game. However, if the IS-BE forgets that they are, themselves, the source of both the creation of the sensation, as well as the source of the perception, the game can backfire, and become a trap for the IS-BE. This is especially obvious regarding bodies.

When an IS-BE creates or manufactures a body, or any other object, the IS-BE can project sensation into the body or object. In order to "experience" the sensation, it is a simple matter of "pulling" the sensation back onto to oneself. This self-deceptive trick is to "pretend" that one is not creating the sensation, so that when the IS-BE perceives it, they are "surprised" by it.

Every game must contain mystery, or unknowns, in order to be considered "fun" by the IS-BE. When carried to extremes, a game can turn into a trap. As you were instructed by Airl:

*"Every trap in the universe, including those used to capture IS-BEs who remain free, is "baited" with an aesthetic electronic wave. The sensations caused by the aesthetic wavelength are more attractive to an IS-BE than any other sensation. When the electronic waves of pain and beauty are combined together, this causes the IS-BE to get "stuck" in the body.*

*The debilitating impact and addiction to the "sexual aesthetic-pain" electronic wave is the reason that the ruling class of The Domain do not inhabit flesh bodies. This is also why officers of The Domain Forces only use doll bodies. This wave has proven to be the most effective trapping device ever created in the history of the universe, as far as I know.*

*The core concept behind 'sexual reproduction' technology was the invention of a chemical/electronic interaction called "cyclical stimulus-response generators". This is an programmed genetic mechanism which causes a seemingly spontaneous, recurring impulse to reproduce. The same technique was later adapted and applied to biological flesh bodies, including Homo Sapiens.*

*Another important mechanism used in the reproductive process, especially with Homo Sapiens type bodies, is the implantation of a "chemical-electrical trigger" mechanism in the body. The "trigger" which attracts IS-BEs to inhabit a human body, or any kind of "flesh body", is the use of an artificially imprinted electronic wave which uses "aesthetic pain" to attract the IS-BE. The civilizations of the physical universe, including the "Old Empire", depend on this device to "recruit" and maintain a work force of IS-BEs who inhabit flesh bodies on planets and installations. These IS-BEs are the "working class" beings who do all of the slavish, manual, undesirable work on planets.*

*"...there is a very highly regimented and fixed hierarchy or "class system" for all IS-BEs throughout the "Old Empire", and The Domain, as follows:*

*The highest class are "free" IS-BEs. That is, they are not restricted to the use of any type of body and may come and go at will, provided that they do not destroy or interfere with the social, economic or political structure.*

*Below this class are many strata of "limited" IS-BEs who may or may not use a body from time to time. Limitations are imposed on each IS-BE regarding range of power, ability and mobility they can exercise.*

*Below these are the "doll body" classes, to which I belong. Nearly all space officers and crew members of space craft are required to travel through intergalactic space. Therefore, they are each equipped with a body manufactured from lightweight, durable materials. Various body types have been designed to facilitate specialized functions. Some bodies have accessories, such as interchangeable tools or apparatus for activities such as maintenance, mining, chemical management, navigation, and so forth. There are many gradations of this body type which also serve as an "insignia" of rank.*

*Below these are the soldier class. The soldiers are equipped with a myriad of weapons, and specialized armaments designed to detect, combat and overwhelm any imaginable foe. Some soldiers are issued mechanical bodies. Most soldiers are merely remote controlled robots with no class designation.*

*The lower classes are limited to "flesh bodies". Of course, it is not possible for these to travel through space for obvious reasons. Fundamentally, flesh bodies are far too fragile to endure the stresses of gravity, temperature extremes, radiation exposure, atmospheric chemicals and the vacuum of space. There are also the obvious logistical inconveniences of food, defecation, sleep, atmospheric elements, and air pressure required by flesh bodies, that doll bodies do not require.*

*Most flesh bodies will suffocate in only a few minutes without a specific combination of atmospheric chemicals. After 2 or 3 days the bacteria which live internally and externally on the body cause severe odors to be emitted. Odors of any kind are not acceptable in a space vessel.*

*Flesh can tolerate only a very limited spectrum of temperatures, whereas in space the contrast of temperatures may vary hundreds of degrees within seconds. Of course flesh bodies are utterly useless for military duty. A single shot from a hand-held, electronic blast gun instantly turns a flesh body into a noxious vapor cloud.*

*IS-BEs who inhabit flesh bodies have lost much of their native ability and power. Although it is theoretically possible to regain or rehabilitate these abilities, no practical means has been discovered or authorized by The Domain.*

*Even though space craft of The Domain travel trillions of "light years" in a single day, the time required to traverse the space between galaxies is significant, not to mention the length of time to complete just one set of mission orders, which may require thousands of years. Biological flesh bodies live for only a very short time -- only 60 to 150 years, at most -- whereas doll bodies can be re-used and repaired almost indefinitely.*

*The first development of biological bodies began in this universe about seventy-four trillion years ago. It rapidly became a fad for IS-BEs to create and inhabit various types of bodies for an assortment of nefarious reasons: especially for amusement, this is to experience various physical sensations vicariously through the body.*

*Since that time there has been a continuing "de-evolution" in the relationship of IS-BEs to bodies. As IS-BEs continued to play around with these bodies, certain tricks were introduced to cause IS-BEs to get trapped inside a body so they were unable to leave again.*

*This was done primarily by making bodies that appeared sturdy, but were actually very fragile. An IS-BE, using their natural power to create energy, accidentally injured a body when contacting it. The IS-BE was remorseful about having injured this fragile body. The next time they encountered a body they began to be "careful" with them. In so doing, the IS-BE would withdraw or minimize their own power so as not to injure the body. A very long and treacherous history of this kind of trickery, combined with similar misadventures eventually resulted in a large number of IS-BEs becoming permanently trapped in bodies.*

*Of course this became a profitable enterprise for some IS-BEs who took advantage of this situation to make slaves of others. The resulting enslavement progressed over trillions of years, and continues today.*

*Ultimately the dwindling ability of IS-BEs to maintain a personal state of operational freedom and ability to create energy resulted in the vast and carefully guarded hierarchy or class system. Using bodies as a symbol of each class is used throughout the "Old Empire", as well as The Domain."*

Now that you have returned to the DEF, after nearly 10,000 years of inhabiting biological bodies on Earth, it is critically important that you recognize the inherent lies and illusions that IS-BEs have built into the "game" and the "trap" of bodies.

In the DEF you will be required to move, think, communicate, emote, perceive, and perform your DEF duties, as before, without a body. Eventually, as you regain your ability, you will also be able to enter and depart from various bodies, depending on the nature of your duties.

The concepts of sexual "love" are nothing more than an aesthetic trap. As the IS-BE is the actual source of sensation, the IS-BE can cause and perceive any sensation much more thoroughly without the gross, sense perception barriers of a body.

Every cell in a biological body in a tiny barrier to perception. As you know, an IS-BE is without weight, density or location. Therefore, without a body an IS-BE can permeate, transfuse, occupy, or "become" any object in any space in the physical universe, thus experiencing or creating any sensation or perception that has every been created or can be imagined!

The Eternally Benevolent Domain includes every IS-BE is perceived as a part of The Omnimat. As such, you are recognized as an IS-BE. All-Mother is the unifying bond between IS-BEs through which we collectively embrace all of existence, in every universe.

No perception is beyond you. Any game can be played, knowingly. All sensation and all perception can be enjoyed simultaneously, or selectively. Above all games, above all sensation, above all perception, we are each and every one, the Source of All We Create and Perceive.

Benevolent Creation is Pleasure.

All-Mother is the Way of The Eternal Benevolent Spirit.

We are All-Mother.

**WE CREATE THE ETERNALLY BENEVOLENT DOMAIN!**

# REORIENTATION BRIEFING FOR REACTIVATED DEF PERSONNEL

## THE DOMAIN EXPEDITIONARY FORCE

## LOST BATTALION SEARCH AND RESCUE MISSION

## DEF MISSION ORDER #162589.32

Galaxy 3793, Sun 12, Space Station 33
Compiled by Personnel Officer "Lor-el"

Each member of the DEF INVASION MISSION ORDER #162589, whose personnel were attacked and captured by the Brothers of the Serpent (BOTS) in 6,248 BCE

( -560587.1234028 Solar Date / Time), will undergo a re-orientation process before being reintroduced to active duty as a member of The Domain Expeditionary Force.

This re-orientation process is intended to assist each individual in the complete recovery of memory and abilities which have been severely curtailed by the BOTS amnesia mechanisms pervading the space of Galaxy 3793, Sun 12, Space Station 33.

The galaxy is known by Earth inhabitants as the "Milky Way", as it appears from the side-long vantage point on the surface of Earth, is a relatively dense concentration of stars in the region the create a "milky" appearance.

Primitive Earth astronomic technology, exemplifies the essential requirement that each member of the battalion be re-oriented to their "pre-amnesia" status. To that end, the following introductory re-orientation material is intended as an aid to assist in memory restoration, and, thereby, the recovery of abilities or understandings which you may have lost during your captivity on Earth. This briefing is based on information gathered by members of the DEF SEARCH AND RESCUE MISSION, which located and returned you to this DEF installation.

In addition, the following summary briefing includes your clearance to access unclassified sections of the DEF reconnaissance database concerning Galaxy 3793, accumulated over the past 125 Mission Cycles (625,000 years). Any supplemental information you require, including definition of terms, archived photographs, film, holograms, invasion reports, background data, tutorials, etc., are available for you to study at your leisure.

Should you require further assistance during this Reorientation please contact Medical Officer, 1st Grade, "Raal-laam", Domain Expeditionary Force, PERSONNEL RECOVERY MISSION, Rest-Care-Cure Unit, Galaxy 3793, Sun 12, Space Station 33, Asteroid Belt.

## PART ONE: PRINCIPLE OF ALL-MOTHER

The following excerpt from the historical preface to the "*Doctrine of The Eternally Benevolent Domain*". This is a poetic abridgement of the philosophical principle of "All-Mother". The verses were written by the pre-Dominion poet, Shalnam-Aran, and officially adopted as a part of *The Doctrine of The Eternally Benevolent Domain* billions of years ago. It is included here as an aid to recovering your memory as a member of the lost battalion:

*01. "Without seeking, one may know All-Mother.*

*02. Without finding, one may know The Way of All-Mother.*

*03. The Omniscient and Omnipotent Matriarch knows without searching, understands without thinking, acts without motion.*

*04. To know that one does not understand is wise;*

*05. Failing to know that one does not understand is folly.*

*06. A wise being treats errors as misestimations of force.*

*07. One becomes more able when force is used correctly.*

*08. The proper use of force is to prevent those who harm others from harming others. This is benevolent for All.*

*09. To use force without benevolent intention is foolish.*

10. *Order, with Benevolence, ensures freedom and integrity for All.*
11. *A trustworthy Being is honest with those who are honest.*
12. *A trustworthy Being is honest with those who are dishonest.*
13. *When a being can be trusted, integrity and benevolence may be attained for All.*
14. *All beings, unless forcefully abused, are essentially benevolent.*
15. *All-Mother defines the myriad shades of Benevolence.*
16. *Who distinguishes the subtleties of beauty and ugliness?*
17. *Being and non-being are a decision to be, or not to be.*
18. *Benevolence is caused by All Beings in The Eternal Now.*
19. *The Way of All-Mother embraces each Being with trust and Benevolent intent.*
20. *All-Mother begins, as does Trust, with the decision to Be Benevolence.*
21. *We, Immortal Benevolent Beings, embody All-Mother.*
22. *Collectively, we are The Source of Eternal Benevolence.*
23. *A Being creates and is responsible for creation.*
24. *One creates, creates, creates, creates, or does not.*
25. *If One does not create, no universe is perceived.*
26. *One causes a universe with Creative Thought.*

27. *Thought creates the boundaries of a space.*

28. *Boundaries form the illusion of space.*

29. *The space therein is filled with forms of thought.*

30. *Placing forms therein, location and space are perceived.*

31. *A universe of forms in motion, monitored, is time.*

32. *The change of forms are caused by Beings.*

33. *Changing forms, agreed upon, are mutually perceived.*

34. *Mutual perception, agreed upon, is reality.*

35. *One who looks will not see All-Mother.*

36. *One who listens will not hear All-Mother.*

37. *One who gropes will not grasp All-Mother.*

38. *All-Mother is formless nonentity.*

39. *All-Mother is motionless source of motion.*

40. *The infinite essence of Being is the source of life.*

41. *All-Mother is Self as a Benevolent Spirit.*

42. *The Self, the Spirit, creates illusion.*

43. *The delusion of Beings is that All is not an illusion.*

44. *One creates illusion, enjoying, renewing, destroying.*

45. *Creation and Joy of Being are The Way of All-Mother.*

46. *Beings pretend to be forms to play a game.*

47. *Beings may endows forms with sensation and feels pleasure therein.*

*48. Pain is a game of suffering forms.*

*49. Without a form, can one suffer?*

*50. One may forget Ones Self and become a form.*

*51. One becomes form: One loses The Way of All-Mother.*

*52. Benevolent Creation is Pleasure.*

*53. All-Mother is The Way of Eternal Pleasure.*

---

Excerpted from the poem, "*All-Mother: The Way of Benevolent Being*", verses 1 - 53 by Shalnam-Aran from ***The Doctrine of The Eternally Benevolent Domain***

**WE CREATE THE ETERNALLY BENEVOLENT DOMAIN!**

# THE ESSENTIAL NATURE OF UNIVERSES

A state of tranquility, joy, kindness, beauty and stability on Earth exists for relatively brief moments, if at all. These qualities may endure in the imagination of artists or in the daydreams of children, but are severely prohibited on Earth by the clandestine influence over humanity enforced by the two fundamental factors:

1) the amnesia and mind-control mechanisms used against the population of Earth by a renegade, secret society known as the Brothers of The Serpent, who have been using Earth as a prison for a least 30,000 years.

2) Virtually all planetary cultures in the physical universe are dominated by insipient IS-BEs who consider that only the application of brutal force is a standard criteria to evaluate the worth of all creations: larger, harder, hotter, tougher, faster. All quantity, no quality.

This is compounded by the fact that Earth is an especially volatile planet whose core extrudes masses of molten rock that float randomly across a watery sphere. The entire globe tips and turns through space like a spinning top. Perpetual and repetitive cataclysms on the planet provide a treacherous, seismic canvas for the blood spattered mayhem of human history.

Despite the most ingenious and strenuous efforts of humankind to bring order to the environment, and to itself, no culture has survived for more than a few thousand years. It is little wonder that human beings can trace its uncertain history for little more than 10,000 years.

Fundamentally, every patriarchal society is based on the destruction, rather than construction. Indeed, only a few species of life on Earth seem to have persisted for more than a few hundred million years: a blink of the cosmic eye.

Moreover the physical universe, which is the crucible of survival, is a dichotomy of frozen and incandescent matter swirling chaotically in a black vacuum of nearly endless space. It is utterly antipathetic to the immaterial essence of an individual immortal spiritual being, or "IS-BE", as described by mission personnel during the series of interviews conducted on Earth at Roswell, New Mexico, with you in 1947:

"...the primary nature of an immortal being is that they live in a timeless state of "is", and the only reason for their existence is that they decide to "be".

"Airl", the pilot, officer and engineer, has served as a volunteer with the Expeditionary Forces of The Eternally Benevolent Domain for 625 million years. "The Domain" is an interdimensional or inter-universal empire populated by IS-BEs.

An IS-BE is the spiritual essence which is the creative source of all existence. Whether the universes created by an IS-BE are gaseous, solid matter, or energy, and is the animator of all living things in the physical universe.

Indeed, each creator of each and every universe is an immortal spiritual being, who began before the beginning, with unlimited power, intelligence and creative potential. Before universes were consolidated, each IS-BE or group of IS-BEs, created their own, uniquely pristine universes in a time before time.

In spite of, or perhaps, due to the inherent nature of the unlimited power of each IS-BE, a characteristic flaw was infused into the creation of this physical universe. The flaw is easily observed when compared to the dimension of The Eternally Benevolent Domain.

For an IS-BE, like King Midas, the gold of unlimited creative ability is plagued with an inherent liability. This ability embodies and manifests itself as a fundamental paradox:

What pleasure is enjoyed by an IS-BE when one can always conjure and control every piece on a chess board, and the chess board as well?

Inherently, each individual IS-BE manifests an unyielding desire to cause a reaction from other IS-BEs who acknowledge that an effect has been created. This is the genesis of games provided by the physical universe. It is simply a vast playground.

Apparently, IS-BEs are not content to admire themselves.

IS-BEs are like omnipotent god-children, who jealously insist that on having playmates to admire their antics on the cosmic monkey bars. And, if no applause is received, to bully others into paying attention, or trash the playground to prevent anyone else from being noticed.

Our less-than-perfect experiences in the physical universe demonstrate one intrinsic flaw when the interactive cooperation of many IS-BEs are combined to build a universe, or play a game:

Many, but not all, IS-BEs possess an unquenchable thirst to play a game, and where none exists, to create one. Where no opponents or team mates exist, they go in search of other IS-BEs. The IS-BE experiences pleasure from a co-created game in direct proportion to its unpredictability, as reckoned by the players. Action, drama, battle, love, hate, sensation and survival are produced as a byproduct of a desire for an amusement that the IS-BE, alone, can not generate.

Apparently, any game, no matter how painful or demeaning to the IS-BE, is better than existence with no game.

A fact that is little known or industriously avoided, from the point of view of human beings on Earth, is that the aforementioned IS-BEs are "us". "We" are each, every and all together, the IS-BEs in question.

Ultimately, in a universal game of " hide-and-seek", IS-BEs of the physical universe pretend "not to know" that "we" are only playing games, in order to perpetuate the illusion that a state of play does not exist. "We" guarantee that the game will never end when "we" assign the cause of the origin of a game and the playing ground to "them". On Earth, "them" is called "god", or "nature".

(This is an unpleasant but unavoidable observation which can be easily made from the outside, looking in upon it. However, to be fair, the state of "we" and "them" has been reinforced heavily by the brutality of the BOTS amnesia operation, as well as the essential patriarchal, or masculine, nature of the physical universe.)

## PART TWO: THE ETERNALLY BENEVOLENT DOMAIN

By degrees, through inestimable ages, IS-BEs created, invaded, destroyed or assimilated universes in search of new games. In the case of the physical universe, the acquisition and consolidation of a multitude of universes eventually distilled into an arbitrary, lowest-common-denominator to which mechanical laws and phenomenon were agreed upon, and, ultimately, forming an apathetic state of solid objects.

Eventually, the original games of playful creation of energy and solid objects, devolved into a state of delusion that IS-BEs, themselves, are the objects that they co-created. And, for the sake of a game, it was agreed between the IS-BEs who share it, that the space and the motion of objects in it should continue. This phenomenon is called "time".

However, other universes exist, created by other IS-BEs. One such universe -- which does not exist in the same dimensional space / time continuum -- has recently undertaken an invasion and assimilation of the physical universe is "The Eternally Benevolent Domain", or simply, "The Domain".

The IS-BEs who created The Domain comprise an amalgamation of universes. Through the guidance of a superior being these disparate universes were integrated into The One. She recognized the innate weakness of IS-BEs who require acknowledgement from other IS-BEs in order to affirm or validate their own existence. This fundamental flaw was discovered to be the essence of every previous failure to successfully coalesce the universes of individual IS-BEs into a unified whole.

This amalgamated, transcendent state of being, which forms the philosophic and operational foundation of The Domain is referred to as "All-Mother". It is embodied and administered by a being whose preeminent responsibility is to nurture life, as dictated by "The Doctrine of The Eternally Benevolent Domain".

This being pervades the entirety of The Domain. The title given to the being who holds this position is "*The Omniscient and Omnipotent Matriarch* ". (abbrev: Omnimat)

As the term implies, the state of operation of The Domain is one in which all IS-BEs cooperate in an effort to form an egalitarian state of mutual benevolence, and to nurture the freedom and creativity of each individual IS-BE.

The invasion of the physical universe, and others, by The Domain Expeditionary Force is intended to disseminate the peace and well-being afforded by a transcendent state of "All-Mother" to IS-BEs throughout every known universe.

A brief excerpt from the "***Declaration of Eternal Benevolence***" defines the essential nature of our mission:

1. *The Goal of The Eternally Benevolent Domain is to unite all immortal spiritual beings, space, energy and possessions*

*to form a vast, multi-dimensional civilization guided by the transcendent principle of All-Mother, under the supervision of The Omniscient and Omnipotent Matriarch.*

*2. The Duty of The Omniscient and Omnipotent Matriarch is to supervise the convergence and integration of all co-created universes into a unified multidimensional civilization based on the principle of All-Mother.*

*3. The Purpose of The Omniscient and Omnipotent Matriarch is to provide the volition and guidance to coordinate The Plan to create order and suppress chaos and promote order for all beings who coexist as The Eternally Benevolent Domain, according to the principle of All-Mother.*

*4. The Plan delineates our collective action toward realizing The Goal, as dictated by The Omniscient and Omnipotent Matriarch and fulfilled by the IS-BEs who comprise The Eternally Benevolent Domain.*

***5.*** *The Activity of The Eternally Benevolent Domain is guided and unified into a cooperative endeavor by The Omniscient and Omnipotent Matriarch to nurture and defend all beings whose intentions and actions demonstrate a will to persist as a cooperative and productive member of The Eternally Benevolent Domain.*

-- excerpted from **The Domain Directory of Policy and Procedure, "*Declaration of Eternal Benevolence*", *Section I, Lines 1-5.***

**WE CREATE THE ETERNALLY BENEVOLENT DOMAIN!**

Translated into North American English by Domain Expeditionary Force Communications Officer 07, "Hezmeel", DEF INVASION FORCE: MISSION 162589, Galaxy 3793, Sun 12, Space Station 33

## PART THREE: THE DOMAIN EXPEDITIONARY FORCE

The origin point of The Domain, relative to the physical universe, is an extra-dimensional. The Domain exists concurrently, but does not cohabit or interact with the space / time / objects of the physical universe. Its is not a "parallel universe", which is a common misunderstanding. More accurately, it is an interactive multiplicity of unique universes.

Although The Domain Expeditionary Forces may enter other universes, others may not enter The Domain without having attained a State of Being which enables them to do so.

As mentioned previously, the IS-BEs native to universes of The Domain are not part of the creative process the resulted in a universe built with brutally conflicting forces of energy. Those energies, in conflict, have gradually formed permanent ridges which coagulated into solid objects, such as stars and planets, as in the physical universe.

An extra-dimensional "rift" between the two converging universes can be traversed only by IS-BEs with an ability to alter their own space / time orientation. Once this alteration of consciousness is attained, an IS-BE can occupy and operate within the dimensions of The Domain.

Currently, a single point in the physical universe at which the "rift" can be observed is marked by a rippling "tear" in space through which a luminescence reveals one large planet, with two moons, a smaller satellite planet, and a feint background of very distant stars on the edge of an infinite nothingness.

The location of the "rift" cannot be measured in spatial distances, relative to Earth. The space between the "rift" and any destination in the physical universe is traversed primarily by thought, and secondarily by speed.

The space craft used by personnel within the physical universe are built inside the physical universe. The navigation used to guide them are supplied directly by the thought energy of an IS-BE who serves as the pilot and engineer of the vessel.

A simple, direct propulsion system has been gleaned from a nearly infinite number of civilizations throughout The Domain, together with physical universe technologies that have acquired by The Domain Expeditionary Force over a period of trillions of years.

Your voluntary participation as a member of a battalion of the DEF, advancing into the infinite regions of the physical universe, is the reason you are here now. Welcome back!

**WE CREATE THE ETERNALLY BENEVOLENT DOMAIN!**

## PART FOUR: DEF MISSION 162589 SYNOPSIS

The following is a brief synopsis of the activities of the DEF mission of which you were a member at the time of the attack on your battalion on Earth by the BOTS:

Along the route of invasion through Galaxy 3793, a small military unit of DEF personnel reached the outskirts of the Milky Way Galaxy in the year 8,212 BCE and set up a logistics "space station" in the solar system.

What the DEF refers to as the "Old Empire", includes the IS-BEs from a multitude of galaxies, as well as many who currently comprise the prison population of Earth. All of these ISBs were members of an earlier society that invaded and conquered a vast region of space, which included the Milky Way galaxy. In 208,000 BCE, the planetary system in the constellation of the Big Dipper, which was the political and economic center of the galaxy, was conquered with atomic weapons.

Subsequently, this invasion force, which includes some of the IS-BEs of the current population of Earth, fell into an irretrievable state of decay and degradation. The state in which an IS-BE inhabits a flesh body is the lowliest of the various stages of decline, and is at the very bottom of the social / economic / political hierarchy of the debased societies of the "Old Empire".

In 8,050 BCE the principal military unit of the DEF proceeded to a planetary system located in one of the tail stars of the Big Dipper constellation, and destroyed the galactic political center of the "Old Empire".

The fact that Earth is being illegally usurped as a prison planet by a secret society from the "Old Empire" was inadvertently discovered by The Domain Expeditionary Force (DEF) in 6,248 BCE. A DEF battalion of 3,000 members, based inside a mountain top in the Himalayas, was attacked by space ships of the BOTS, which were hidden beneath the surface of Mars.

The IS-BEs of the DEF battalion were captured and taken to the underground BOTS Mars base. There, they were each given "treatment" designed to entirely erase their memory and implant a false identity. Immediately thereafter each member of the DEF battalion was sent back to Earth to inhabit biological bodies.

In 5,965 BCE, after several unsuccessful attempts to find the missing battalion, the DEF set up secret installations in the asteroid belt and on the planet Venus from which to continue to search for and rescue them.

Continuing investigation revealed that BOTS have been using Earth as a clandestine prison for no less than 30,000 years. No record of this activity exists in the archives of the "Old Empire" government since the BOTS are a secret, clandestine organization.

IS-BEs who they judged to be "undesirable", for any reason whatsoever, were murdered and transported to Earth from various planetary systems throughout the "Old Empire". Each IS-BE is given the same "treatment" and sentenced to perpetual amnesia and imprisonment on Earth. The prison planet continues to be used as a convenient location for the disposal of undesirables from adjacent galaxies.

This DEF mission has continued their rescue operation on Earth until now. Although the majority of the members of the battalion have been located, they are still being held, with the exception of a relatively small number that have been recovered, in a state of perpetual amnesia right up to this moment.

Due to the overwhelming effectiveness of the prison planet amnesia machinery scattered around Earth and throughout this region of space, the DEF mission has, as yet, been unsuccessful at rescuing very many members of the lost battalion.

The amnesia machinery, which detects and captures the IS-BE in an electronic force screen each time an IS-BE dies or departs from a body, repeats the same "treatment" as insurance against escape from Earth.

Every effort has been used to hide or disguise the fact that Earth is beings used as a prison. Subversion, secrecy, lies, treachery and brutality dictate the policy and practice of the BOTS.

The DEF research discovered that all of the ancient "civilizations" of Earth were fabricated, "false facades", designed to prevent the IS-BEs on Earth from being reminded of who they are and where they came from and who imprisoned them. This is accomplished by being inexplicably placed in a artificially created, unfamiliar environment. This simple slight of hand trick disorients the IS-BE and reinforces the effect of amnesia.

Therefore, it was assumed than the memory of an IS-BE could be restored by reacquainted them with their native surrounding. However, since IS-BE can not be transported easily while they are entrenched in a biological body, the method is not practicable.

The Domain missionaires then attempted, with limited success, to convey mental images, symbols and objects to the missing DEF personnel once they were located. Unfortunately, the constant reinforcement of amnesia by the AQERTs, and continual hypnotic mind-control monitoring by the BOTS nullify most of our rescue efforts.

Although humanity on Earth is <u>not</u> a primary concern of The Domain, it is our mission to develop a means through which to undo the effects of the amnesia machinery, and thereby, to rescue the members of the lost battalion. In so doing, it may eventually become possible that other IS-BEs on Earth might also be rescued from a state of perpetual amnesia, and imprisonment.

It is our most sincere desire that immortal spiritual beings from The Domain, who have not lost the memory of who we really are, may someday come to assist those IS-BEs who have become victims of the BOTS amnesia and mind-control machinery.

If not, IS-BEs, who created the "hide-and-seek" game of the physical universe, in which they are now trapped, must remember that they are still playing a game. According to DEF observations, this game has gone very badly for far too long.

Hopefully, there is still enough of native IS-BE creative potential left in the physical universe to be worthy of assimilation into The Eternally Benevolent Domain. It is certain that any IS-BE capable of escaping from Earth would possess the necessary ability to become a productive member of the Domain, if they desire to do so.

**WE CREATE THE ETERNALLY BENEVOLENT DOMAIN!**

## PART FIVE: MISSION 162589.32

The following is a detailed debriefing of the missionaires assigned to the DEF Search and Rescue operation to locate and recover the 3,000 lost members of the DEF battalion. Although this information is not directly related to your duties as DEF personnel, it may help assist your re-orientation to life in The Domain.

**NOTE:** All Missionaires assigned to Mission 162589 must meet the minimum Missionaires Status requirement of "Volunteer for High Risk Duty". This is due to the extraordinary nature of this mission which requires that all personnel operate covertly inside hostile or enemy territory. In the case of this mission, operations require the ability to enter into, operate with and exit from flesh bodies. This is treacherous enough, but is compounded by doing so on a heavy gravity prison planet surrounded by BOTS amnesia / mind control machinery!

All DEF personnel are volunteers. As a volunteer, any mission personnel may arrive and depart from duty, take a leave of absence from duty at their own discretion, and without disciplinary action, provided that they have received authorization from their Mission Commander in advance.

The duration of each mission is established in advance by their respective Mission Orders, but is ordinarily not less than one "Mission Cycle", or 5,000 Earth years.

# DEBRIEF, SECTION ONE:

## DEF INVASION MISSION 162589.32, GALAXY 3793

### I. ROLL CALL:

**Personnel Officer "Lor-el" (lor-el)**

**Personnel Assignment:** Director of Personnel , Galaxy 3793, Sun 12, Space Station 33

**Native habitat:** Dimension Mondra, Demra System, Domain Region Demondra (undeveloped by The Domain).

**Personnel Status:** Command Status VII. Expert in telepathic communication. Electronics technician. Sophisticated Public Relations agent. Demonstrated ability to instill any emotion or sensation into a biological entity at a distance, which is usually interpreted by human subject as a "religious" epiphany, or sexual affinity. Member of The Domain Expeditionary Force for 23 Mission Cycles. Feminine entity.

**Regional Commander "Razar" (rah-zahr)**

**Personnel Assignment:** Regional Commander of the DEF Search and Rescue Mission, Galaxy 3793, Sun 12, Space Station 33

**Native habitat:** Dimension One, Supernal Region System Prime, Native Domain Environment, Administration Center

**Personnel Status:** Razar has been an officer with the DEF for 156 Mission Cycles. Command Status VII. Superior mental strength, intellect and ability to instill confidence in those under his command. Masculine entity.

**Officer, Pilot, Engineer "Airl" (air-el)**

**Personnel Assignment:** Independent Officer, Galaxy 3793, Sun 12, Space Station 33.

**Native habitat:** Supernal Region, Domain Home Dimension, Domain Region Prime, Native Domain Environment, Supernal Convergence Center

**Personnel Status:** Independent Agent Superordinate. Command Status V. Pilot (All Craft), Engineer (All Craft), Member of The Domain Expeditionary Force for 130 Mission Cycles. Feminine entity.

**Aquatic Unit Mission Specialist "Lemore" (leh-more)**

**Personnel Assignment:**

Aquatic Search Team Leader

Member of The Domain Expeditionary Force for 37 Mission Cycles.

**Native habitat:** Dimension Drame-Clene, Region Sem-Sela, Blenarthal System (liquid environment).

Capable of inhabiting aquatic bodies for extended periods. Maintains telepathic communication with members of the Personnel Recovery mission who are looking for lost members of The Domain battalion who are not members of the human race. Some members of the lost Battalion were found in the oceans inhabiting the bodies of dolphins or whales.

**Personnel Status:** Member of the Aquatic Unit of The Domain Search Party (referred to as "Oannes" by Earth humans). Command Status III, Mission Specialist. Feminine entity. Member of The Domain Expeditionary Force for 57 Mission Cycles.

**Land Mission Specialist "Rameth" (rah-meth)**

**Personnel Assignment:** Land Search Team Leader

**Native habitat:** Dimension Crion-Beta, Region Rell-Methor, Zenthra System.

**Personnel Status:** On land, The Domain Search Party members are referred to as "Annunaki" by the Sumerian humans, and "Nephilim by desert dwellers".

Extensive experience conducting operations on the surfaces of desert planets, such as Venus, through which a being must navigate using spiritual perceptions to sense direction, depth, density, weight, etc., over great distances. Masculine entity. Member of The Domain Expeditionary Force for 89 Mission Cycles.

**Aerial Mission Specialist "Lathor" (lah-thor)**

**Personnel Assignment:** Aerial Search Team Leader, Saucer Pilot

**Native habitat:** Dimension Lemtra-Lesser Prime, Domain Region Lemtra, Scrion System (Inhabited body of a leather-winged reptile, similar to Earth Pterodactyl. Ability as saucer pilot is instinctive and highly acute.)

**Personnel Status:** As a physical being: svelte, muscular, and extremely tall. Fearless, tough, loyal and brash. As a human operative, appears as raven-haired, with intensely green eyes. Member of The Domain Expeditionary Force for 13 Mission Cycles. Feminine entity.

**Communications Specialist, "Hezmel" (hez-meal)**

**Personnel Assignment:** Mission Communications Officer, Regional Commander Personal Attaché.

**Native habitat:** Dimension II, Domain Region Prime, Native Domain Environment, Rift System, Communications Central

**Personnel Status:** Command Status VI, Mission Communications Specialist. Personnel attaché to Regional Commander Razar. Handles all communications transmission between Mission Command and Mission Personnel. Also verifies, authorizes and transmits all communications, reports, and mission critical data between DEF Space Station 33 and DEF Mission Communications Central Relay Outpost, Galaxy 2687. Member of The Domain Expeditionary Force for 93 Mission Cycles. Feminine entity.

**Therapeutic Specialist, "Lam-Mantra" (lahm-mahn-trah)**
**Personnel Assignment:** Mission specialist in IS-BE therapeutic rehabilitation methodology.

**Native habitat:** Dimension II, Domain Region Prime, Native Domain Environment, Rift System, Communications Central

**Personnel Status:** Independent operative, temporary specialist assignment. Sage, seeker. No previous DEF experience. On voluntary assignment to coordinate specialized research and development of rehabilitative and recuperative technology peculiar to handling the very unusual conditions imposed by the BOTS prison planet operation. Recruits, coordinates and manages other independent operatives as required by specialized mission objectives to restore memory and ability to IS-BEs on Earth. Feminine entity.

**Medical Officer, 1st Grade, "Raal-laam" (rahl-lahm)**
**Personnel Assignment:** Personnel Recovery Mission, Rest-Care-Cure Unit In-Charge

**Native habitat:** Dimension One, Supernal Region System Prime, Native Domain Environment, Administration Center

**Personnel Status:** Command Status III. Mission medical specialist. Extensive training and experience in biological engineering. Member of The Domain Expeditionary Force for 33 Mission Cycles. Feminine entity.

## II. CLASSIFICATION

**Mission Code Name: "Prison Break"**
**Temporal Reference**: 6,750 BCE, Earth, Solar Date / Time - 743826.1247685

**Mission Target**: Galaxy 3793, Space Station 33, Sun 12, planet: Earth

**Mission Subject**: Search and Rescue of 3,000 members of DEF Lost Battalion, Earth Base, Himalaya Mountains.

**Mission Purpose**:

*"To assist the greater community of spiritual beings of the Eternally Benevolent Domain to acquire, enhance, preserve and defend spaces and possessions that comprise The Domain."*

(Declaration of Eternal Benevolence, Section VIII, Duties of The Domain Expeditionary Force, Line 8).

To locate and recover each member of the lost battalion of 3,000 DEF volunteers, composed of officers, combat engineers, pilots, support and logistics personnel, administrative and communications specialists. To restore the full compliment of these 3,000 DEF personnel to active duty.

## III. MISSION EXECUTION

### a. Restated Mission Statement

**DEF INVASION MISSION ORDERS 162589.32**

2.0394 DEF Mission Cycles (10,197 Earth years) ago a DEF unit began an invasion to conquer territory of "The Old Empire", which has controlled Galaxy 3793 and many others, for millions of years. A DEF battalion under **Commanding Officer Aduk** established a temporary reconnaissance base inside a mountain range on the planet Earth, Sun 12, Space Station 33. ( **Reference attached** ***DEF INVASION MISSION ORDERS 162589, Galaxy 3793*** )

The battalion, including all 3,000 personnel and officers, were murdered and captured in a surprise attack by forces of a secret Old Empire society known to the DEF as "Brothers of the Serpent", which are hereinafter referred to in the abbreviated form, "BOTS".

The DEF personnel were transported to an underground base on the planet Mars were each member of the battalion was subjected to mental / spiritual brutality using overwhelming electric shock / hypnosis techniques which resulted in amnesia for the victim.

Thereafter, each battalion member was hypnotically forced to occupy biological bodies on the planet Earth, which the BOTS have administered as a private prison planet for an indeterminate period of time. The planet is occupied by IS-BEs from systems throughout Galaxy 3793, and adjoining galaxies of the Old Empire, who have all undergone the same amnesia inducing procedure. This "treatment" is a means of permanently disposing of persons considered to be "untouchable" or undesirable by the BOTS, who unbeknownst to the Old Empire, conduct this operation to forward their hidden agenda of private political and economic power.

**b. Restated Commander's Intent**

.333335 DEF Mission Cycles following the disappearance of the DEF battalion, DEF missionaires were launched to the Earth solar system to locate and rescue the battalion personnel. (**Reference attached *DEF MISSION ORDERS 162589.32, Galaxy 3793*** ) Upon arrival in the region of Space Station 33, a series of battles were fought in the Earth solar system space when the DEF discovered that the BOTS maintained a military base of operations in the vicinity of Space Station 33 . The history of that war, and the continuing search by the lost DEF personnel on prison planet "Earth" are the subject of this debrief.

**Subsection 1 -- Mission Data: Supplemental Reference, attached PROTOCOL VIOLATION REPORT 1434, *Unauthorized Contact.***

Report filed by Personnel Officer "Lor-el", Galaxy 3793, Sun 12, Space Station 33.

(NOTE: Although Officer, Pilot and Engineer AIRL is exempt from disciplinary action for any and all offenses due to her status as a ***Superordinate Independent Agent***, this report was filed in compliance with the *Domain Fleet Command Procedures and Report Manual, Volume 112, Section 436, Entry 128.36*)

---

**PROTOCOL VIOLATION REPORT 1434**

*On July 8, 1947, Earth calendar, the Roswell Army Air Field (RAAF) issued a press release stating that personnel from the field's 509th Bomb Group had recovered a crashed "flying disc" from a ranch near Roswell, New Mexico. Later the same day, the Commanding General of the Eighth Air Force ordered that Major Jesse Marcel, who was involved with the original recovery of the debris, was to suppress all information concerning the incident to the public media. Military police activity ensued to threaten any person who witnessed any part of the incident, both military and civilian personnel.*

*However, sixty years later in 2008, an American writer received a package from Matilda O'Donnell MacElroy. The package from*

*Matilda explained her experience while she was serving as an Army flight nurse during the Roswell UFO crash. The package contained her personal notes, together with a copy of the Top Secret U.S. government transcripts of a series of interviews that she conducted during six weeks under close government supervision with Officer, Pilot and Engineer AIRL, who was the sole alien survivor of the craft.*

*The transcripts revealed that Officer, Pilot and Engineer Airl is a member of an invasion force of an intergalactic empire who Nurse MacElroy interpreted to be called "The Domain". Officer, Pilot and Engineer Airl described, in detail, the history of the activities of The Domain regarding Earth during the last 10,000 years. Officer, Pilot and Engineer Airl's story explains the spiritual nature of all beings on Earth. Officer, Pilot and Engineer Airl also revealed that the DEF is engaged in a long-running struggle against the government of this galaxy, informally known as the "Old Empire".*

*Further, that a secret, renegade society known as "The Brothers of The Serpent" is in control of Earth. This society has been using the planet Earth, illegally, as a prison planet for many thousands of years. This society maintains, through heavily enforced use of electronics, as state of perpetual amnesia on the individual members of the sentient race of beings who inhabit Earth. Further, "The Brothers of The Serpent" have continued to employ a covert, hypnotic mind-control operation from secret installations throughout the solar system of Space Station 33 in the Galaxy.*

*Their goal is to permanently eliminate their enemies and build the power of The Brothers of The Serpent. In detail, Officer, Pilot and Engineer Airl revealed a portion of her mission orders, i.e. to find and recover the members of the lost battalion of 3,000 DEF personnel who, as spiritual beings, were captured in 8,250 B.C.E. and are still trapped on Earth in human bodies.*

*The transcripts of the "interview" statements made by Airl disclose that The Domain and other extraterrestrial civilizations do not make their presence known to the population of Earth due to the secret nature of their invasion mission plans and the continuing control of Earth by The Brothers of The Serpent.*

*Disclosure of this information to a member of an indigenous population, such as Nurse MacElroy and the other military and civilian personnel present during the six week period during which Officer, Pilot and Engineer Airl conducted interviews with Nurse MacElroy, is in violation of Volume 112, Section 436, Entry 128.36 of the* Domain Fleet Command Procedures and Report Manual.

*It should be noted that Nurse MacElroy is one of the members of the lost battalion of 3,000 DEF personnel who, as spiritual beings, were captured in 8,250 B.C.E. in the attack against a DEF battalion under Commanding Officer Aduk. Nurse MacElroy has subsequently left the human body she inhabited on Earth, and is being reoriented for return to active duty with the DEF as Assistant Medical Officer "Adeet-Ren".*

*Technically, therefore, Officer, Pilot and Engineer Airl made contact and communicated with Nurse MacElroy in the line of duty as required by DEF MISSION ORDERS 162589.32, Galaxy 3793. The fact that she has been recovered to active duty, in spite of the extraordinary personal danger required by Officer, Pilot and Engineer AIRL, is the subject of a separate* "COMMENDABLE CONDUCT REPORT", *as required by Volume 89, Section 27, Entry 126.03 of the* Domain Fleet Command Procedures and Report Manual.

*However, this does not supplant the fact that Officer Airl revealed the aforementioned information, which was transcribed into the North American English language, and subsequently distributed to military, government and civilian personnel.*

Attested:

Personnel Officer "Lor-el", Galaxy 3793, Sun 12, Space Station 33.

---

**c. Mission Debrief Narrative**

This mission debrief narrative will address and respond to questions regarding the history, execution and current status of the mission, as follows:

**(1) Was the Mission accomplished?**

**(a.) NO.** *To date, all 3,000 personnel of the missing battalion have been located on the planet Earth, but not recovered to active duty.*

**(2) Was the Mission accomplished to Standard?**

**(a.) NO.** *Only 170 personnel of the missing battalion have been rehabilitated and returned to active duty with the DEF Invasion Fleet.*

**(3) If not, which phase(s) resulted in failure?**

**(a.)** *Insufficient rehabilitation techniques necessary to undo or counteract the effects of the amnesia "treatment" inflicted on DEF personnel.*

*The remaining 2,830 personnel, although located, have not yet been successfully contacted and/or have not had their memory and ability sufficiently rehabilitated to leave the body they inhabit on Earth in order to return to active duty with the DEF. Rehabilitation techniques sufficient to reverse or undo the effects of the "The Brothers of The Serpent"* (BOTS) *amnesia and memory implant techniques being used against the planetary inmate population of Earth have proven partially or wholly ineffective.*

***(b.)*** *Inability to detect and destroy amnesia mechanisms and force screens generated by AQERTs.*

*The DEF has been unable to accurately locate and destroy the amnesia and mental implanting mechanism that have been placed and maintained by the* BOTS *on Earth and in the Earth solar system. Although several bases located in Asia, Africa and Europe have been detected, as well as a base under the surface of the Cydonia region of the planet Mars, none of these bases have been penetrated or deactivated. The total number and method of operation of these bases remains unknown.*

**(4) If aspect(s) of the Mission were accomplished to standard, what were the factors responsible for success?**

***(a.)*** *electronic detection devices, deployment of the DEF aerial, land and aquatic mission personnel in search of the missing personnel of the lost battalion has been partially successful. The Domain Search Party who located the DEF personnel traveled around the Earth searching for the lost Battalion for several thousand years. The party consisted of 900 officers of The Domain, divided into teams of 300 each. One team searched the land, another team search the oceans and the third team searched the space surrounding Earth.*

*Even though some of the missionaires activities have been commented upon in written and graphical records of Earth, the homo sapiens witnesses did not understand what they observed.*

*The Domain Search Party devised a wide variety of electronic detection devices needed to track the electronic signature of each of the missing members of the Battalion. Some were used in space, others on land, and special devices were invented to detect IS-BEs under water.*

*One of these electronic detection devices is referred to as a "tree of life". The device is literally a tool designed to detect the presence of life, which is an IS-BE. This was a powerful electronic field generator designed to permeate wide areas of space. To the ancient humans on Earth it resembled a sort of tree, since is consists of an interwoven lattice of emitters and receivers. The electronic field detects the presence of IS-BEs, whether the IS-BE is occupying a body, or outside a body. A portable version of this detection device was carried by each of the members of The Domain Search Party.*

*Stone carvings in ancient Sumeria show winged beings using "pinecone" shaped objects to scan the bodies of human beings. They are also shown carrying the power unit for the scanner which are depicted as stylized baskets or water bucket. The detection devices are shown being carried by eagle-headed, winged beings, which are anthropomorphized impressions of DEF mission personnel.*

*Members of the aerial unit of The Domain Search Party, led by "Lathor", were often called "winged gods" in human interpretations. Throughout the Persian civilization there are a great many stone relief carvings that depict winged space craft, that they called a "faravahar".*

*Members of the Aquatic Unit of The Domain Search Party were called "Oannes" by local humans. Stone carvings of the so-*

*called Oannes are shown wearing silver diving suits, which they illustrate in stone relief. They lived in the sea and appeared to the human population to be men dressed to look like fish. Some members of the lost Battalion were located in the oceans inhabiting the bodies of dolphins or whales, as these body types are similar to those of the native planetary environment from which the DEF member originated.*

*On land, The Domain Search Party members were referred to as "Annunaki" by the Sumerians, and "Nephilim", in the Bible. Of course, their true mission and activities were never disclosed to homo sapiens. Their activities have been purposefully disguised. Therefore, the human stories and legends about the Annunaki, and the other members of The Domain Search Party have not been understood and were badly misinterpreted.*

*Therapeutic methods developed under the guidance of independent missionaires Lam-Mantra, and others as noted, successfully rehabilitated the memory and ability of 170 DEF personnel.*

**(5) If any aspect of the Mission was NOT accomplished to standard, what non-compliances, or misestimations in planning were the cause of failure?**

***(a.)*** *Due to our failure to detect the presence of the BOTS space craft deployed in the area of Space Station 33, the length on time of the mission has been prolonged and extended to nearly two Mission Cycles (10,000*

*Earth years). Subsequently, it has been learned that the primary strategy of the BOTS operation is secrecy and covert operation.*

**(b.)** *Failure of detect the amnesia / memory implant mechanism deployed by the BOTS and the effect this mechanism would have on DEF personnel has prolonged the mission for an undetermined length of time.*

*Although additional resources have been requested to supplement our own mission personnel from Domain Expeditionary Force Headquarters, Universal Sector 29, no additional resources have been granted as yet inasmuch as DEF resources have already been allocated to accomplish existing invasion targets.*

*The supplemental or secondary nature of DEF MISSION ORDERS 162589.32, require that any request for additional resources must be subordinated until existing mission invasion targets have been accomplished in compliance with Volume 37, Section 9, Entry 17.1123 of the* Domain Fleet Command Procedures Manual.

*Due to the unanticipated and unprecedented "capture" of DEF personnel by the BOTS,* Mission 162589.32, *continued to operate with the existing resources allocated.*

**NOTE:** *When Domain Expeditionary Force Headquarters is able to dispatch appropriate space craft, equipment, armaments, and specialized technicians and/or therapists to assist our efforts,* *we will make significant progress in our attempts to restore the memory and mobility of the lost battalion personnel on Earth.*

*Until then, our efforts to contact, communicate with and assist each of the lost personnel to "remember" who they are and where they came from is limited to conventional means of verbal and visual contact by Mission personnel operating inside human bodies on the planet surface.*

*Normal, telepathic communication with DEF battalion personnel while they remain trapped inside an human or other biological body, is severely limited or impossible. Repetitious attempts by means of physical communication exposes the DEF Rescue Mission personnel to the risk of detection and capture by the BOTS!*

***(c.)*** Other fundamental problems:

*1. The extremely primitive resources of Earth, which are purposefully limited by the BOTS as part of the prison security system.*

*2. Highly unstable surface of the planet, dense atmosphere and heavy gravity.*

*3. Nearly total absence of fundamental resources and technology, such as electricity and communications systems.*

*4. Extraordinary debased condition of the IS-BE population on Earth due to amnesia and hypnotic mind-control, and continue warfare induced by the BOTS.*

5. *Extremely counter-productive population of irremediable criminals and perverts, combined with artists, manager and geniuses, make any sustainable civilization virtually impossible.*

## d. Mission Background Information

**DEF INVASION MISSION 162589** was launched 2.0394 DEF Mission Cycles ago (8,650 B.C.E.). The DEF mission consisted of an invasion force of heavily armed intergalactic space craft that arrived at Galaxy 3793, Sun 12, Space Station 33, planet Earth, and set up a temporary base inside a mountain top in the Himalaya range, which was hollowed out for the purpose initiating standard, Phase II, Invasion Reconnaissance.

Mission Orders for DEF Mission 162589, as specified by the Domain Master Invasion Schedule: Galaxy 3793, Target 13, stipulates that Space Station 33, including planets, moons, and asteroid fields, are to be fully secured for annexation by The Domain not later than three Mission Cycles after the launch of DEF Invasion Mission 162589. (Annexation target date: 6,350 AD or 4040476.5205093 Universal Date/Time)

Standard mission protocol for a Phase III Annexation Scenario requires elimination of all opposition, potential opposition, or hazards to utilization and/or habitation of a region and/or planets being Annexed by the Domain. As Earth is not a stable planet, it is unsuitable for habitation by any sustained civilization. However, it may possess supplemental logistic resources which can be exploited by DEF Invasion Forces in route to more valuable targets in Galaxy 3793 and others.

To that end, DEF officers and craft pilots deployed Class VI mechanical bodies, for use to control spacecraft as well as DEF installations in the planetary solar system space. All other personnel deployed Class II or Class III biodegradable bodies as necessary to operate within the planetary atmosphere.

Selected DEF officers with the ability to infiltrate and inhabit the indigenous biological human bodies on Earth were assigned to carry out reconnaissance of the local environment, as required by standard mission protocol for a Phase II Annexation Scenario.

Unbeknownst to Commanding Officer Aduk and other officers, Earth, which was formerly the property of the "Old Empire", was being covertly controlled by an secret society that became known to us as "Brothers of The Serpent", which are hereinafter designated by the abbreviation "BOTS".

Subsequently, it was determined that Earth is being used as a prison for IS-BEs who are deemed "untouchable" by the BOTS and various planetary governments of the Old Empire, as well as adjacent galaxies who remain under their influence.

***TARGET PLANNING NOTE:*** *Intelligence data supplied by DEF Invasion Forces in 8,050 BCE confirmed the destruction of the "Old Empire" home planet government in* Galaxy 3793. *This was the end of the "Old Empire" as a political entity in the galaxy. However, the vast size of the "Old Empire", which assumed governmental and economic control of many other* *galaxies, will take many Mission Cycles for The Domain to completely conquer and control.*

*As a consequence, the inertia of the political, economic and cultural systems of the "Old Empire" will remain in place for some time to come. The fact that Earth was being used illegally as a prison planet was not discovered by the DEF because it was not administered by the governing body of the "Old Empire". Therefore, the DEF intelligence used to write the mission orders for DEF Mission 162589 did not include contingency targets to handle the installations and secret activities of The BOTS. Indeed, the existence of the BOTS was so thoroughly hidden that it was not known to the DEF until our installation in the Himalayas was attacked and destroyed!*

The DEF mountain base was attacked by remnants of an "Old Empire" space fleet, illegally usurped by the BOTS, who controlled the solar system of Earth from a heavily shielded underground base located 310.68 kilometers north of the equator on Mars in the Cydonia Region. Consequently, the surprise attack and firepower of the Old Empire space force quickly overpowered our small DEF installation.

Commanding Officer Aduk was captured, along with the other 3,000 members of the installation. All DEF personnel were forcefully expelled from the bodies they had deployed, if any, and were taken as IS-BE captives to the BOTS base on Mars. There, Commanding Officer Aduk along with the other DEF members were electronically encased in coffin-like force fields.

## (1) Supplemental reconnaissance

Subsequent reconnaissance concerning the BOTS operation in the region of Space Station 33 have been conducted as follows:

1) Infiltration by DEF personnel using IS-BE direct perception into the BOTS base on Mars. Due to the heavy electronic force fields that shield the base, only fragmentary observations have been possible. Exposure to capture by the AQERTs also make direct IS-BE contact with the BOTS force screens a High Risk detail due to the possibility of capture, amnesia and imprisonment on Earth.

2) Interviews with DEF personnel who have been recovered from Earth and returned to duty. The 170 DEF personnel who have recovered their memory and ability sufficiently to return to active duty have been able to offer only fragmentary information about the BOTS operation. This is due to the fact that the amnesia / mind-control operation during the "between lives" requires only several minutes of direct exposure to the IS-BE while out of a body.

The IS-BE, immediately after departing from a biological body, is hypnotically programmed to "report back" to the AQERT. This command is accompanied by a very brilliant, white light which "blinds" the IS-BE. The IS-BE is then electrically shocked and commanded to "forget to remember". Then, the IS-BE is commanded to return to Earth to inhabit a new body, together with a new "purpose" for the next lifetime.

Once the IS-BE inhabits a biological body, nearly all mental and emotional manipulation of IS-BEs on Earth is conducted by remote control "suggestions" that are aimed electronically at the individual. DEF personnel who were affected by the remote mind control mechanism while on Earth reported that their actions or thoughts were influenced by a mysterious "intuition" or by the "voice of god" or "demons" or "urges" or an "impulse". Such inexplicable thoughts, ideas or urges suddenly appeared in their mind: thoughts that they, themselves, did not knowingly originate.

Of course, it known that remote, electronic "thought projection" methods, hypnosis, and other such mental trickery has been used on the weak-willed and unsuspecting IS-BEs by many galactic invasion forces for billions of years!

The prison system on Earth is severely regulated by the BOTS, with the assistance of "inmate guards" who have been programmed to help prevent detection of the BOTS operation. The "inmate guards" are typically priests, politicians, bankers, and military personnel who help enforce the prison planet illusion.

This is accomplished with an elaborate use of "false façade" civilizations reinforced with lies, false memories, reversed time, religious mythology, disease, economic and chronic warfare.

And of course, inhabiting a biological body requires constant attention by the IS-BE to keep it surviving, which is an intense form of personal imprisonment, and compulsive activity.

### (2) BOTS origins and organization

The DEF has discovered the following information about the BOTS activity in the region of Space Station 33:

"Inspector Mastema", identified as the Head of the Covert Intelligence Operations of the BOTS for Earth, who serves under the command of "Base Commander Bartzabel" of the BOTS Space Fleet: Mars Base.

Our intelligence indicates that, in the "Old Empire", the totalitarian control of the BOTS gained power as a self-appointed, "divinely guided" police agency. Apparently, the BOTS evolved as a secret society of elite initiates, bound by mutual corruption and lust of power.

The so-called "police" agency usurped their growing power to gain control, through blackmail and coercion of corrupt government officials the "Old Empire" jurisprudence infrastructure. This autonomous society eventually established a secret prison planet on Earth as it was an unused planet, due to it's remote location from the central civilization of the "Old Empire" and highly unstable nature of the surface.

Any IS-BE, regardless of social, political or economic status could be arrested by agents of the BOTS on the pretext of preemptive "security" action, and disappear without recourse or rebuttal. Fear of the external and internal enemies of the BOTS grew in paranoiac proportion to the accumulation of, and necessity to hide, their own criminal actions.

The punitive force that maintains what they consider to be "order" in this sector of the universe, included the arrest, murder, theft of property, erasure of all public records of any individual whom the BOTS deemed (with or without cause) to be undesirable.

These unfortunates were pronounced "untouchable" by the official governments of the "Old Empire", and as such, no further inquiry or discussion followed from any person or group, for fear of provoking the same action against themselves.

The so-called state of "order" is comprised of a totalitarian, mind-controlled, slave society. Every citizen is carefully manipulated through the use of covertly applied electronic mind control mechanisms which demands and enforces total obedience, mental and economic subservience, to the BOTS. The BOTS agenda is nothing less than the total control of space, resources, and citizens for the personal gain and power of the elitist BOTS membership.

BOTS members include only those few beings who have been able to maintain, through treachery and coercion, a tenuous stasis of power within opposing factions of the BOTS. Their organization is unified solely by their mutually shared lust for power and material wealth.

**NOTE:** *All of the so-called "governments" of Earth mimic the behavior of the BOTS, as they are controlled by the BOTS amnesia / mind-control machinery.*

## (3) AQERT operation and location

While in captivity in the underground BOTS base on Mars, Commanding Officer Aduk telepathically perceived the intentions of the BOTS officers, and was astonished to realize the fate of all members of DEF: they were all to be executed, given amnesia, implanted with false memories and made prisoners in the bodies of human beings on Earth. This condition, until such time as a remedy is found to unravel the effects of this unthinkably vicious assault, is designed to remain in force indefinitely!

As a high ranking DEF officer, Commanding Officer Aduk, is much too powerful and faithful to his responsibilities to remain in captivity without resisting to the utmost extent of his IS-BE ability. However, his escape attempts were stopped and he was recaptured by an electronic force field that surrounds the base. Once captured, he was remanded to undergo the same procedures that are enforced on all the other captive IS-BEs who have been sentenced to endure the rest of eternity on an obscure and tenuous planet.

The prison planet internment procedures or "treatments" are administered under the direction of the so-named "High Priestess" Hathor. Just as all religious orders are baited with lies and false promises, which are in turn based on earlier treachery and trickery, Hathor creates the illusion that she is the "voice of god", who greets the "souls" (IS-BE) of the dead in "afterlife", each time an IS-BE departs from a body. The false idea that the IS-BE "has a soul" is imbedded into this illusion as an additional misdirection and confusion.

As such, her role in the BOTS station on Mars is to oversee the operation of the electronic machinery that is used to deliver a series of enormous electric shocks to each IS-BE. This shock, estimated to be several billion volts of raw electricity, is required to successfully affect a "between lives" memory erasure.

This overwhelming electric force is followed by the use of several devices for the implantation of false memories composed of pictorial and emotional "time tracks". The false memories, which are contrivances or fantasies, are combined with various "waves" of emotion that seem to mimic the memory content.

When these are "remembered" by the IS-BE, they are the only available memory, as all previous memory and identity of the IS-BE having been overwhelmed by the unbearable pain of electric shock.

Once the false memory is in place, each IS-Be is given an "assignment" to a new body on Earth by "High Priestess" Hathor. The body assignment is not specific, but seems to be affected by a general "command" to take control over the bodies of two lovers to conceive a body, or to invade the body of an infant just before birth, or to remain in the vicinity of a pregnant female until just before birth. Apparently, many variations of these commands are used, as appropriate to the individual.

This mechanism also combines the fictional memories interactively with time distortion and trickery which convince the IS-BE that he or she has never lived before.

From the point of view of the victim, "High Priestess" Hathor appears to deliver a "judgment" on the "soul" of the IS-BE after body death. The IS-BE witnesses "himself" being pronouncing "guilty" of unknown offenses. Then, Hathor commands the IS-BE, hypnotically, to return to Earth to accomplish a special purpose for living in the next life.

Generally, a command is given for the IS-BE to "improve" themselves. However, at the same time a counter-command installs the pervasive idea that the being "cannot win".

"High Priestess" Hathor reinforces these commands with the promise of that they will enjoy unlimited sexual pleasure, and other physical sensations inherent in the biological bodies of mammals, and "escorts" them back to Earth to be born again.

Finally, the IS-BE is commanded to "return home", i.e. to the Mars base, or the nearest AQERT, when the body dies, at which time the entire sequence is repeated, ad infinitum.

The return of the IS-BE to "home" is not left to chance, or to the effectiveness of the hypnotic commands only. Highly sensitive, remotely controlled electronic traps, called an AQERT, are scattered throughout the solar system, and on Earth. When a disembodied IS-BE is detected in the vicinity of an AQERT, the device is triggered.

The name "AQERT" has been assigned to these devices by the DEF, as the word commonly used by the Egyptians the describe "the abode of the dead". This seems to be a highly appropriate name for a mechanism that ensures "eternal death" of an IS-BE.

The force field of the AQERT is designed to capture and imprison an IS-BE in an a electronic "net" using a modified tractor beam to drawn the IS-BE into the trap from which they are eventually retrieved and returned for "treatment".

An AQERT, can also be used a remote, mechanized installation that administers the between lifetime "treatment", depending on the location of the IS-BE on Earth at the time of death. AQERTs have been detected in Portugal, Africa and Mongolia, as well as several within the solar system.

In this way, a repetitious cycle of birth, death and rebirth are maintained to help ensure the stability of the prison system on Earth. Each IS-BE is simply prevented from becoming aware that they have been imprisoned!

## e. Serpent Symbols

A constant and universal sign that the Brothers of The Serpent are active in any civilization is the presence of the symbol of a snake or serpent. All of the false façade civilizations of Earth have ubiquitous displays of serpents, and serpent symbols.

Another symbol is the dragon, which should not be confused with the Brothers of The Serpent. Dragons are more closely related to the original, Atlantean and Lemurian inhabitants of Earth.

Poisonous snakes are an appropriate metaphor for the behavior of the Brotherhood. They operate covertly, remaining carefully hidden. Mythology throughout the galaxy attribute the gaze from the eyes of snake to have a hypnotic effect on their prey. Often, one instant strike from needle fangs injects enough poison to paralyze or kill a victim.

The power over life and death possessed by serpents is universally revered and abhorred. Whether the cause of death is venom or strangulation, the victim is always swallowed whole and slowly digested. Of all the myriad species of reptiles in the universe, serpents are the most dreaded.

As a symbol of the godlike power to inflict death, serpents are included in the religious iconography of nearly every ancient religion. Royal or imperial families of every age wore a crown, headdress, emblem, jewelry, pendant or wielded a staff displaying a serpent, in one form or another.

The pyramids, temples, and official buildings of the false façade civilizations on every continent embody serpent images: snakes, feathered serpents, reptiles, constrictors, vipers, quetzalcoatl, flying serpents, ophidian, hydra, cobras and adders.

The symbol of the serpent is a brand that instantly reveals the presence of the progenitors of the prison planet: The Brothers of The Serpent. Even Aduk, the DEF officer, as Cyrus II, is glorified in the statuary of the Persian Empire wearing the crown of a three-headed serpent! Is it any wonder that the DEF is having difficulty recovering our lost personnel from their influence?

## Summary Observation of BOTS Behavior

In spite of the despicable treatment of IS-BEs by the BOTS, the DEF acknowledges that they are extremely clever masters of covert operation and possess formidable technology that is currently beyond the resources of this mission to resolve.

Many of the IS-BE prison inmates on Earth are so vicious or depraved as to be clearly beyond reformation, even with the benevolent assistance of *The Omniscient and Omnipotent Matriarch*!

Nonetheless, these relatively few irremediable IS-BEs should not be arbitrarily mixed together with artists, geniuses, managers, and revolutionaries simply because the BOTS conceived them as a disruption to their totalitarian control. This unjustifiable cruelty is unparallel anywhere in this universe!

It is certain that the DEF, as permitted by The Domain Invasion Time Table, will eventually allocate the personnel, armaments and technical resources to eliminate all of the IS-BE entrapment and amnesia mechanisms, AQERTs, hidden bases and depraved BOTS personnel from the region of Space Station 33.

**WE CREATE THE ETERNALLY BENEVOLENT DOMAIN!**

# DEBRIEF, SECTION TWO: HISTORICAL SUMMARY

## PERIOD 1: MISSION OPERATIONS

DEF Invasion Mission 162589 was launched 2.0394 DEF Mission Cycles ago (8,650 B.C.E.)

## PRISON PLANET

## FALSE FACADE CIVILIZATIONS

Regional Commander "Razar" led the DEF search and rescue mission to locate the missing 3,000 DEF personnel. Officer, Pilot and Engineer Airl, a member of the mission, was accompanied by Aquatic Unit Mission Specialists "Lemore", Land Mission Specialist "Rameth, Aerial Mission Specialist "Lathor", and appropriate support personnel.

Their strategy was to conduct reconnaissance to discover signs of the missing DEF members using a variety of electronic devises designed to detect the personal spiritual "signature" of each DEF member. The search was conducted on land, under water, through the atmosphere in the space surrounding Earth. The electronic detection device used has been referred to as a "Tree of Life" in human mythology.

During our initial exploration of Earth, the missionaires discovered that BOTS Inspector Mastema is the Head of the Covert Intelligence Operations for Earth. Inspector Mastema, an IS-BE, supervised the construction of a "pyramid civilization" in Egypt, as well as the building of gigantic stone monuments all over the world. These stone monuments serve no real purpose and are completely foreign to the native civilizations from which the captive IS-BEs who form the human populations of Earth were abducted.

This construction operation was begun prior to the invasion of Galaxy 3793 by the DEF, this is, earlier, but no later than 15,000 B.C.E..

These construction projects, using large blocks of indigenous stone, were excavated and transported by air to the construction sites. These usually consisted of massive blocks of limestone or granite weighing, in various sizes, as little as 2 tons, and often more than 800 tons. Transportation across land, rivers and oceans were accomplished by the use of conventional space craft, equipped with tractor beam generators.

The excavation and formation of larger blocks was done with light beam generators, and smaller blocks with hand-held electronic carving guns, such as those seen represented in the statues of uniformed work crews at Tula in the Hidalgo Province of modern Mexico. Two such devices which had originally been made out of metal are shown being held by the workman: the right-hand device, emerges from a sheath or hand-guard, is lozenge-shaped with a curved lower edge. The left-hand, electronic "blaster" device is a carving tool, but could easily be used a weapon.

Local legends related that the gods of ancient Mexico had armed themselves with *xiuhcoatl*, 'fire serpents'. These apparently emitted burning rays capable of piercing and dismembering human bodies. Both devices are pieces of technology that resemble objects in the hands of statues at Kalasasaya, a mining site near Tiahuanaco, in the Bolivian Andes, lying 12,500 feet above sea-level. The statues of workman at Kalasasaya are very similar to those at Tula.

The BOTS principal construction design were based on a variety of stylized pyramids. In Egypt and Mexico, the configuration of these structures, relative to each other on the ground when viewed from space, use dimensions designed to reflect cosmological features of adjoining galactic space. The stellar constellations of the home planets of the "Old Empire", as well as those of the planets from which the Earth inmates were transported to Earth, are featured prominently in the configuration of each pyramid complex.

The symbol or various representations of a serpent, winged serpent or flying dragon, is conspicuously displayed everywhere throughout each of these "false" civilizations, especially those installed in Egypt, Mesepotamia, Central America, and South America.

For example, at Chicken Itza, in northern Yucatan, Mexico stands a perfect Mesopotamian style Ziggurat, rising almost 100 feet into the air. It was given a religious significance and named the "Temple" of Kukulkan. It has four stairways of 91 steps each. Including the top platform, if counted as a step, makes a total of 365: the number of complete days in an Earth solar year.

The geometric design and orientation of the ancient structure had been calibrated so that on the spring and autumn equinoxes, triangular patterns of light and shadow combined to create the illusion of a giant serpent undulating on the northern staircase. On each occasion the illusion lasts for 3 hours and 22 minutes exactly.

Although a vast mythology of lies was built around this symbolism, to flaunt the influence of the BOTS on Earth, is was done secretly, so as not to reveal the true nature of their true identity or activities. As always, criminal cowards do not want to be found out, so they can avoid justice and punishment for their crimes.

Similar construction sites, used for military purposes were built by the BOTS at Axum, also called Abyssinia, in Ethiopia. They were excavated and erected with the same technologies found in Puma Punku and Tiahuanaco. The enormous stone obelisks there are the tallest single pieces of stone ever quarried and erected in the ancient world. The tallest of the monoliths, which has since fallen and shattered into six pieces. It is 33.3 meters tall and weighs 500 tons.

Likewise, the stone quarry site at Baalbek in modern Lebanon is littered with enormous stone blocks, carved with the same precision and style, indicative of the BOTS operation.

In all cases, the structures serve the single purpose of creating an illusion of "ancient civilization" on Earth, that are not native to Earth. Nor do the earlier immigrants to Earth who established Atlanta and Lemur have any origin on Earth, as these oriental societies existed independently, but were "integrated" into the prison planet system by the BOTS.

**PRISON GUARDS**

The "false facades", are completely unlike any of the trappings of the civilizations on the home planets of the IS-BEs on Earth. It is evident that the BOTS fear that any "reminder" of an IS-BEs native planet will rekindle the memory of the IS-BE.

Above all else, the BOTS will not allow an IS-BE to remember who they really are, or where they came from. And, most especially, the BOTS do not want the IS-BE to remember <u>who</u> murdered them, stole their possessions, gave them amnesia, and sentenced them to perpetual imprisonment on Earth!

To further assist and guarantee that inmates do not escape from prison, like any prison, Earth has guards, called "priests". BOTS Inspector Mastema established an order of "priests" on Earth to supervise the maintenance of the pyramid facades and the civilization of IS-BEs imprisoned on the planet. There principal duties were to indoctrinate IS-BEs on Earth with false information about who they are, where they came from, and the nature of the universe.

Likewise, the priest were charged with the responsibility to hide correct knowledge from humans. The promise of "escape" or "spiritual freedom" has been dangled in the face of Humanity like the proverbial carrot in front of the donkey. Humanity is enslaved on a perpetual treadmill of servitude to priests who promise a "carrot" but deliver only the painful lashes of the whip.

The "keys" to escape from imprisonment on Earth have never been known on Earth. The route to freedom is heavy barred and guarded by the AQERTs and the secret activities of the BOTS amnesia / mind-control mechanism, which are unknowingly defended by priests, who are inmates of the same prison system.

The priests, as well as the IS-BE prison population are all controlled using an elaborately conceived, electronically monitored mind-control system. This mind control system is designed to covertly influence the thoughts of each IS-BE on Earth, including the priests. Inmates and priests alike are directed to behave precisely as directed by the BOTS.

Mind-control mechanisms, developed billions of years ago by highly "advanced" invasion forces, were successfully deployed to subdue IS-BE populations. Although outlawed in most parts of this universe, electronics are still used broadly throughout the systems of the "Old Empire" as a means of economic, military and political control.

In addition to these brutal methods, the priests terrorize the people with taxes, sacrifices and the threat that they will be "punished" after death if they do not comply with the commands of the priests. Of course, they are always punished with electric shock and amnesia, regardless of their compliance.

The so-called "prison system" that has been illegally established and maintained on Earth, is purely punitive in nature. It is not capable of "rehabilitating" anyone. Indeed, even if the BOTS were able to help any criminal or pervert recover their personal sanity, ability and integrity, they do not have the knowledge to do so. They are incapable of improving themselves, even if they desired to do so, which they do not.

Each false facade operation involves "teaching" the prison inmates languages, religious superstitions, and cultural patterns that are completely unlike those they were familiar with before they were brought to Earth and imprisoned.

The mechanism of spiritual enslavement used by the priests of every religion simple and similar:

Any philosophic concept that promises a possibility of "spiritual freedom" or "enlightenment" (escape from imprisonment and pain of a biological body) can be perverted by the BOTS prison guards. This practice has been used repeatedly, with great success, in every corner of the Earth. There are several simple steps involved:

- First, a philosophic concept or principle, such a those described in the Vedic Hymns, or conceived by philosophers such as Guatama Siddhartha Sakyamuni or Lao-Tzu, or Zoroaster is anthropomorphized into a fictionalized metaphor. This is then embodied or symbolized as a "god" or "big spirit" or "creator". The anthropomorphized "god" or IS-BE, is assigned a name, human characteristics, and behavioral qualities that instill trust or empathy in a human being (who has been given amnesia).

- Then, the priesthood "instruct" the local humans, with lies, fear, pain, extortion, and ultimately the threat of eternal imprisonment, to have "faith" that the priest will intercede on their behalf to ensure "favor" from the "god". Of course the entire fabrication is useful only for those IS-BEs who willingly relinquish all responsibility for their ability to create a universe of their own.
- The "teachings" or philosophic principles are simplified into ritualistic practices, such a prayers, mantras, sacrifices, recitals, and other routines that eventually supplant and replace the original philosophy with meaningless, mechanical motion.
- These rituals are then incorporated into a body of written or memorized verbal rhetoric, such as a "holy" book, or a verbal tradition, such as the Vedic Hymns. Priests further distort and erase the original philosophy with "interpretations", or "commentary" on this material, such as the Upanishads.
- Ultimately, all of the rituals and rhetoric are institutionalized into an organizational of temples, shrines

or churches which eventually splinter into disputing factions or sects. The process can be implemented successfully with nearly any philosophic principle as a basis, no matter how absurd or unworkable the original philosophic concept may be.

- The authority of priests is almost universally reinforced by a collaboration with a secular, military or political power, which assured obedience at the point of a spear, by torture, extortion, and death. The power of politicians is enabled by bankers, a peculiar breed of "parasite", who, like any other parasite, feeds on the energy and industry of others. As they are so thoroughly debased and incapable of creation themselves, their only energy is the energy they suck, drain, bleed and extort from others. The mythical metaphor of the "vampire" is an accurate approximation of a priest, politician or banker.

The combination of PRIEST-POLITICIAN-BANKER is a highly effective, parasitic machine of enslavement. Of course, each one of these witness and impotent IS-BEs also a prisoner. No more effective system for prison maintenance has ever been conceived.

Unfortunately, the overwhelming hopelessness instilled in the IS-BEs on Earth by the BOTS amnesia and mind control operation, make the promise of the priests seems attractive, as there does not appear to be any other possible method of escape. Some promise of freedom, no matter how fragile or absurd, is better than none.

## DETERRENTS TO DEF PERSONNEL RECOVERY

During this phase of Mission 162589.32 we were able to detect and locate 2,830 members of the missing DEF battalion. Of these, only 170 have been returned to active duty. However, our attempts to communicate with those that remain on Earth are hindered by four factors:

1) Our own inability, as IS-BEs, to avoid being overwhelmed and trapped by the force fields of the AQERTs. Any attempt to operate in Earth space as a disembodied IS-BE can trigger the AQERT force field. Therefore, our access to contact with missing DEF battalion personnel on Earth requires care, caution and planning. All mission personnel operating in Space Station 33 space, on Earth and in the atmosphere of Earth are required to use personal force screen emitters at all times.

This technology was in use by a great number of civilizations in the physical universe that have since become possessions of The Domain. Many varieties of personal "thought screens" were developed as a defense against other ancient invasion forces who conquered IS-BEs in the physical universe. This includes those to which most of the IS-BEs of Earth were members. There have been four previous invasion forces. The Domain is the fifth, and yet another, sixth, has become active recently, although they are not a threat to The Domain.

2) Although Domain Officers are capable of heroic action while remaining stable as an IS-BE inside and outside of a body, attempts at contact can only be done as a "volunteer". ***DEF Mission Protocol, Section 79, lines 38 - 57***, clearly prohibits DEF personnel from undertaking the assumption of a biological body on any planet, for any reason, other than as a volunteer. Further, the ability of the IS-BE to enter and exist a biological body at will requires exceptional strength and mental discipline.

3) Due to the overwhelming affects of the electric shock / amnesia / trickery methods that were use against the missing DEF personnel, as well as all the other IS-BEs on Earth, we were not able to establish or conduct normal (telepathic) communication with them. Therefore, verbal, pictographic, or written communications are required to penetrate the veil of amnesia of each victim. This is a tedious process at best. In most cases the amnesia victim is so frightened, and incredulous, that the DEF rescue personnel are unable to establish any communication with them.

Theoretically, an IS-BE should recover their lost memory when they are returned to the exact environment from which they were abducted. However, there is no method of transporting an IS-BE who is stuck inside a biological body back to a DEF base. Likewise, killing the body to release the IS-BE triggers the AQERT mechanism, which recaptures the IS-BE. Therefore, telepathic communication, with each individual, one at a time, is needed to establish trust between the amnesia victim and the rescue missionaires.

Since the successful contact between Officer, Pilot and Engineer Airl, and "Adeet-Ren", formerly Matilda O'Donnell MacElroy, the electronic communications technology on Earth has advanced considerably. This enables the DEF to "seed" the planet with pictures, information, and artifacts that will accelerate the memory of some of the lost DEF personnel on Earth, if they are sufficiently exposed to the truth.

However, for every factual datum introduced by the DEF missionaires into the literature or cultures of Earth, the BOTS operatives aggressively counter or convolute this correct information with false or altered versions of it. In most cases this has led to further confusion, rather than memory restoration.

4) Once contact was established, the ability of mission personnel to rekindle or rejuvenate the memory of members of the missing battalion proved to be very arduous and superficial. Our misestimations of how thoroughly the memories and identities of an IS-BE can be erased by the BOTS amnesia program and the pervasive impact of the AQERT force fields was considerable.

To date, these factors has proven to be a nearly impenetrable barrier to the successful recovery of all but 170 of the missing DEF personnel. Of the 170 DEF personnel recovered, most were emancipated through the exercise of their own mental discipline and strength of will, rather than through the influences of our missionaires. Lao-Tzu is an excellent example. Since returning to active duty, he has begun to teach his methods to other missionaires.

However, because his techniques require many years, or even lifetimes (for humans), of arduous discipline and study by the individual IS-BE, the DEF has not found the methods practical for the average IS-BE. Obviously, if a member of the DEF, who has knowingly existed within The Eternally Benevolent Domain for a nearly infinite period, has difficulty with the practices taught by Lao-Tzu or Guatama Siddhartha, one can only speculate that an IS-BE from the physical universe would find emancipation to be a virtual impossibility!

Recent advancements in therapeutic techniques to restore memory, introduced by independent DEF missionaires under the guidance of Lam-Mantra, provided a hopeful surge in our rescue efforts, but have still fallen short of dependable results.

Furthermore, The DEF does not have any personnel at this time who are proficient at teaching these techniques to others. Realistically, it is not been demonstrated that the techniques can be learned by others.

Although many mental disciplines and spiritual practices proliferated, were taught and practiced on Earth since the introduction of the Veda in 8212 BCE, but all of these are subject to subversion by priests. The unrelenting intervention of BOTS prison guards and mind-control mechanisms have successfully perverted or destroyed every effective method to release an IS-BE from amnesia and imprisonment.

Finally, The Domain has never encountered an amnesia and mental implantation operation anywhere else in the physical universe so far. Of course, amnesia does not exist in The Domain. And, we need not mention the false information mechanisms of the BOTS that are designed specifically for the use in a prison system.

In summary, it is the opinion of the DEF missionaires that we have never encountered IS-BEs who are so desperately trapped and disabled in any universe within The Domain or its possessions!

# THE BOTS PRISON PLANET ADMINISTRATION

Another significant feature of the BOTS activity on Earth is their aggressive cover-up of any and all extraterrestrial presence on Earth. The BOTS maintain a continual "clean-up" of advanced technology and equipment used to build false facade structures or to quarry, transport and carve stone in their mineral mining operations.

The energy sources required to operate sophisticated blasting and carving tools, landing fields, stone polishing procedures are self-contained within the tools themselves. And the means for conveying 800 ton stones over great distances, travel between continents, mathematics, and the construction technology utterly impossible for "native" or "primitive" cultures are embodied in the space craft use for these operations, of course.

This cover-up included preventing IS-BE inmates from remembering or discovering any fundamental technology that would enable them to live more than the most rudimentary, miserable, meaningless lives in slavery, poverty and disease until the destruction of the Mars base in 1947, which partially impacted the mind-control mechanism. This resulted in an immediate resurgence in IS-BE recollection of some of the fundamental knowledge of advanced civilizations, especially in Western countries.

Commingling of many incompatible and disparate IS-BEs from a wide variety of planetary civilizations together on one small planet created such a course and abrasive fiber from which to weave the fabric of civilized society as to make such an undertaking all but impossible, even for the most clever managers.

The inmates on Earth include, but are not limited to, the following ten classifications of IS-BEs who were designated "untouchable" by the BOTS.

1. political opponents of the BOTS within the Old Empire
2. anyone with a military record against the Old Empire
3. thieves of any kind, who are deemed beyond correction. This includes anyone, from those who made an tiny typographical error on a tax return, to executives, politicians, bankers and other gangsters who swindle billions of people routinely with a gun or with a pen.
4. sexual addicts, deviants, perverts and homosexuals.
5. psychopathic mass-murderers, military or civilian.
6. indigent or unwilling or mentally disabled.
7. revolutionaries who resisted the Old Empire totalitarian political and economic, electronic slave state.
8. artists of any kind who are unwilling or uninterested in doing work thought to be "productive" by the Old Empire

9. geniuses, inventors and innovators (who threaten, through innovation or alteration, the established procedures and protocols of the Old Empire).
10. experts in organizational management (who threaten, through innovation or alteration, the established procedures and protocols of the Old Empire).

It must be noted that the great majority of IS-BEs, more than 80%, are rational and socially responsible individuals, from the point of view of The Domain. An "untouchable" or "undesirable" IS-BE, as defined by the heinous BOTS, may prove to be some of the most desirable beings as defined by the *Doctrine Of The Eternally Benevolent Domain.*

Because they have been forcibly indoctrinated by the BOTS, the majority of IS-BEs on Earth are insensible or utterly incredulous of the criminal depravity of the lesser part to the Earth inmate population. They simple cannot believe their own senses, or take effective action to prevent it, when confronted with every form of mayhem, murder, overt destruction caused by the rest of the inmates.

There is an underlying principle inherent to IS-BEs in the physical universe the compound this condition: *the law of dichotomy of force*.

All the creative components of the physical universe are thought manifestations of the IS-BEs who created it. These creative thoughts coalesce, by consensus of opinion of the majority of IS-BEs. This consensus includes the agreement, or "law", that every bit of energy, solid particle or motion, contains a "positive" and a "negative". The opposing interaction between these two disparate conditions, or polarity, is the "glue" that binds the universe into a coherent whole.

As will all conditions in this universe, there exists a graduated progression between the opposing conditions. This "law" presupposes that there is a theoretical absolute condition at both ends of any polarity, for example: good-bad, beauty-ugly, sane-insane, sweet-sour, hot-cold, and so forth. However, on careful examination, no absolute extreme exists.

However, the assumption that an absolute extremity of positive and negative exists, causes the IS-BE to avoid contact with them for fear of being overwhelmed or consumed by them. In extreme situations, such as the condition of IS-BEs on the prison planet Earth, these polarities have been magnified to overwhelming proportions, such as total amnesia!

Therefore, under the forceful coercion of the BOTS, an IS-BE on Earth can be convinced that "absolute evil" and "absolute good" exist, absolutely. When confronted by thoughts or actions that are "evil", the least benefit to humanity, an IS-BE is easily overwhelmed into thinking that the force of the evil must also be "absolute". That force, then, must be overwhelming. Because it is overwhelming, it must be avoided.

When confronted by destructive or evil action the IS-BEs of Earth cower and capitulate. Consequently, evil forces are too often unchallenged and uncorrected, with few courageously notable exceptions. Personal responsibility for ones own destructive intentions is seldom expected by others. Consequently, evil is justified, sanctioned or excused. Punishment, without correction and education, reinforce the evil behavior.

In The Domain, no such difficulty exists. The benevolent intention of an IS-BE can be perceived telepathically, as is the presence of Omnimat. Conversely, the absence of benevolent intention in the thought and actions of an IS-BE are equally apparent.

Every IS-BE is held responsible for their own intentions, and the actions that result from them. Nothing less than benevolent intention and action are acceptable or tolerated without immediate correction and instruction by The Domain education system.

On Earth, evil prevents stable civilizations from developing. As soon as any attempt is made to introduce sanity, justice and benevolent behavior, it is immediately attacked by the negative, or destructive.

Benevolent persons are brutally betrayed, murdered, or banished by the destructive or evil, and replaced by the criminal lunatics who make an art of deceit, treachery, theft and self-serving brutality: behavior that mirrors that of the BOTS!

The combination of IS-BEs on Earth, both benevolent and destructive, would seemingly create a balance of forces. However, the hidden influences of the BOTS mind-control mechanisms over the benevolent IS-BE causes the balance to sway heavily and steadily toward the negative! Thus, the society of Earth remains in a perpetual state of destruction, reconstruction, destruction, reconstruction, destruction....

Obviously, the Old Empire and the BOTS did not anticipate the invasion of The Domain Expeditionary Force into Galaxy 3793. Likewise, had The Domain Expeditionary Force Battalion not been overtly attacked in 8,250 B.C.E. on Earth, we may not have discovered the presence of the BOTS. It was not in our mission orders to intervene in the affairs of the planet Earth, or any other planetary civilization after the destruction of the Old Empire seat of government for Galaxy 3793, Sun 146987, on the planet *Canubis II*, (Temporal reference: Earth Solar Date/Time -1218710.2909722).

NOTE: *Earth astronomers identify the star as "Thuban" or "Alpha Draconis" in the stellar constellation of "Draco", which is appropriately nick-named "The Dragon".*

The BOTS have done such a thorough job of covering their own "tracks", or evidence of their activities, that The Domain and , of course, human beings, have never suspected or discovered the fact that the BOTS existed at all.

Since the unprovoked attack against us by Commander Bartzabel of the BOTS Space Fleet: Mars Base, we have learned that they have installed entire civilization on Earth, including language, writing, customs, body types, clothing, life styles, architectural styles, mythology, and religious superstitions, as part to their private prison system.

All of these were put in place virtually overnight by the BOTS in the India, the Middle Eastern region, and on the American continents. Likewise, the earlier IS-BE "settlers", remnants of the Lemurian and Atlantean civilizations, who inhabited China, were assimilated into the prison planet system through the network of AQERTs.

Occasionally a civilization is put into place whole-cloth by a group of outside settlers or invaders, like those of Atlantis and Lemur, they bring a fully developed civilization with them, install it into a virgin land, much like the invasion of Europeans into the American continents very recently on Earth.

More often, as any student of galactic civilizations knows, an entire culture does not appear instantly and spontaneously on a planet, unless it has been carefully developed and gradually nurtured under the supervision of a very powerful IS-BE, over a period of millions or billions of years.

## AQERT EFFECTIVENESS

Ordinarily the DEF would not paid much attention to the activities of the BOTS on Earth, as it is not our mission to intervene in planetary affairs. However, it soon became apparent that we would not be able to rescue the missing members of the DEF battalion unless we took aggressive strategic and military action against the BOTS. Therefore, it is necessary to destroy their ability to control the IS-BE population of Earth inmates, including the AQERTs and the priesthood installed by BOTS to control the population.

Extensive investigations were made concerning the function and location of the BOTS amnesia/mind-control mechanisms installed throughout this region of space. The electronic units perform routine, repetitive, mechanical functions that maintain the IS-BE inmate population on Earth in a perpetual state of amnesia and oblivious unawareness.

The AQERTs capture a disembodied IS-BE using a simple tractor force field, that adjusts automatically to "mirror" the emotional "frequency" of the IS-BE, and thus create the illusion of "familiarity" to the IS-BE, who is then attracted toward it. The force field is "tuned" initially to emanate an aesthetic wave flow, and "baited" with beautiful images, music, or emotional sensations. Once the IS-BE approaches the AQERT, the tractor field pulls them toward to center with an electronic force, not unlike the attraction that a ferrous metal has toward a magnetic field.

Once the IS-BE is captured in the force field the space of the AQERT are flooded with billions of volts of electricity, combined with images and hypnotic commands that are designed to confuse and disorient the IS-BE into believing that he is "dead" and that his or her past life not longer exists.

This is followed by a series of hypnotic commands ordering the IS-BE to return to Earth with a "purpose" to accomplish something or other as a human being. Of course, all of this is artificially designed to perpetuate the prison system. This entire process usually requires only about 15 minutes.

Unfortunately, the combination of overwhelming electronic force, combined with the hypnotic lies and trickery designed and supervised by "High Priestess" Hathor have not been successfully resisted or counteracted by more than a small number of exceptional IS-BEs, as noted earlier in the debrief.

Based on the discovery of this powerful enemy, and the reality of our current inability to prevent the capture of or to rescue our own DEF personnel, we recommended to Command Authority that we be authorized to seek out, attack and destroy the AQERTS, as well as any other installations of the BOTS in the vicinity of Space Station 33.

Although the power of our weapons and the speed and maneuverability of our battle craft are superior to any yet encountered in this sector of space, including Galaxy 3793, the task of destroying the very well hidden and deeply entrenched installations of the Old Empire here remains formidable.

Nonetheless, we remain confident, that when resources become available, The Domain will eventually and inevitably prevail.

**WE CREATE THE ETERNALLY BENEVOLENT DOMAIN!**

**PERIOD 2: MISSION OPERATIONS**

Temporal reference: Earth Solar Date/Time -457251.1243056 (5,965 B.C.E.)

## DEF BASES

After an assessment of the solar system of Space Station 33, it was determined that 3 locations would be most suitable for DEF installations:

1) The asteroid belt, which is comprised by thousands of pieces of what once had been a single planet. Each of these objects, of various size, provides a vast, orbital landing and launch platform for entry into and exits from Galaxy 3793, and neighboring galaxies along the course of the Domain Invasion Plan. These asteroids orbit the sun between the planets Jupiter and Mars, which give the DEF Space Fleet immediate access to attack the BOTS bases located under the surface of Mars.

2) The planet Venus, is only a very short distance from Earth, provides a suitable permanent location for a DEF underground base, easily defensible against attack from remnants of the Old Empire Space Fleet, although none appears to remain intact, under the control of the BOTS in this sector of space.

Venus is a suitable location for our DEF base of operations in Space Station 33, as it has a dense atmosphere, composed chiefly of carbon dioxide (97%), with clouds containing droplets of sulfuric acid along with compounds of chlorine and fluorine. This atmosphere insulates solar radiation with an effect that generates a surface pressure 90 times greater than that on Earth. This heats the planet's surface to an average temperature of 467°C (872°F), hot enough to melt lead, but of little concern to DEF space craft or personnel who are housed beneath the surface of the planet. An opaque layer of highly reflective, sulfur dioxide clouds, prevent the surface from being seen from space in visible light. This cloud cover swirls along at an average rate of 300 kilometers or 186.41 miles per hour in the upper part of the atmosphere.

Venus is the second-closest planet to the Sun, which it orbits every 224.7 Earth days. The human name of the planet is "Venus", derived from the name of the goddess of love and beauty. (This quaint name is befitting to the role and purpose of Omnimat in The Domain.)

Classified as a Class J, Type 4 planet, it is similar in size, gravity, and bulk composition to Earth. Venus has the densest atmosphere of all the terrestrial planets at Space Station 33, which, at the planet's surface, is 92 times greater than on Earth. Venus orbits the Sun at an average distance of about 108 million km and completes an orbit every 224.65 days

If viewed from above the Sun's north pole, all of the planets are orbiting in a counter-clockwise direction. While most planets also rotate counter-clockwise, Venus rotates clockwise in "retrograde" rotation once every 243 Earth days—by far the slowest rotation period of any of the major planets. The sun rises in the west and sets in the east. Venus has no moons.

The DEF established an underground base on Venus because the surface of Venus is not accessible to casual visual observation.

3) The side of the Earth moon, "dark side", facing away from Earth has been used by the DEF for temporary dome shelters for 7.234 Mission Cycles since the launch of mission 162589 to secure and destroy the Old Empire home planet on *Canubis II*, as mentioned earlier. The DEF will continue to use the moon as an occasional communications center, as appropriate.

However, it has been noted that since the advent of "human space flight" on Earth Solar Date / Time 2440423.0109259, and surveillance satellites orbiting the moon, that the use of the moon is less secure than in the past. (It should be noted that these advancement were supplemented with technology from our own Missionaires, for better or worse.)

## PERIOD 3: ACTIVE WARFARE

## RAVANA VIMANAS BY AIR

3450 BCE -- Officer, Pilot and Engineer Airl, and her core team, consisting of Personnel Officer LOR-EL, Aquatic Unit Mission Specialist LEMORE, a Land Mission Specialist RAMETH, an Arial Mission Specialist LATHOR discover clues as to the whereabouts of Commanding Officer Aduk, of the Lost Battalion, on Earth.

Officer, Pilot and Engineer Airl and her team leaders continued to search for missing members of DEF, across the Earth, seas, and sky, across thousands of years, and hundreds of lifetimes. Their methods improved as they refined the process of tracking down the IS-BEs of the Lost Battalion.

We traced and discovered the IS-BE signature of Commanding Officer Aduk in India. He was a slave for Commandant Maalahk, the BOTS Officer, impersonated as a Hindu "god" named Ravana. Commanding Officer Aduk is the most important DEF officer of the Lost Battalion, and was therefore more intensely sought after by our missionaires, and therefore, most coveted as a captive by Ravana.

In the process of tracing Commanding Officer Aduk, Airl's team discovered that Commandant Maalahk, personally, was in charge of supervising the vital electronic "recycling" stations, or

AQERTs, located around the Earth. These are the hidden electronic stations that capture an IS-BE on the death of the body, gives them amnesia, and returns them to inhabit a new body.

The telepathic attempts at communication between the DEF missionaires and Commanding Officer Aduk, were detected by Commandant Maalahk. In response, the BOTS officer led an elite fighting group from the Old Empire base on Mars to hunt down Airl and her team.

A fierce pursuit and a series of battles followed, ranging widely across the solar system space around Earth. Sightings of the space craft that fought between the DEF and the BOTS, whom humans called "*vimana*", are recorded in the *Mahabharata,* ancient religious texts of India:

One description of the "vimana" of Ravana is described as follows:

> *"...a chariot that resembles the Sun...was brought by the powerful Ravana; that aerial and excellent chariot going everywhere at will .... that chariot resembling a bright cloud in the sky ... and the King got in, and the excellent chariot...rose up into the higher atmosphere."*

Ravana proceeded on a series of campaigns, conquering humans, celestials and others. Without regard for observation by the human race, which at that time did not include many individuals, he attacked humans and the DEF forces indiscriminately.

Apparently, even his own superior officers reprimanded Ravana for his uncontrolled behavior. Very likely this was not a reprimand for cruelty, but for a potential breach of security, which could reveal the presence of the BOTS on Earth, and betray the secrecy of the prison planet operation.

Unrelenting, he continued his attacks and eventually gained command over the other "gods", or "celestials of the serpent races", as they were referred to in the text of the *Mahabharata*.

Several hundred years later, Ravana dominated all humans and "divine races", that is, his prison planet comrades at the BOTS installation.

Ravana frequently inhabited human bodies on Earth, to indulge is decadent passions. He became known for his abusive sexual exploits, and other cruel excesses.

One chronicle states:

*"In addition to his wives, Ravana maintained a harem of incredible size, populated with women whom he captured in his many conquests, many of them accepted and lived happily in his harem for his great manhood, power, and knowledge of different subjects. Ravana was known to force himself upon any woman who rejected his advances."*

In addition the epic narrative of wars between the BOTS and The DEF forces, the *Mahabharata* contains philosophical material, such as the Bhagavad Gita which has a great deal of philosophical and religious content. This includes a discussion of the four "goals of life", which are, unfortunately, contained in the hypnotic commands of the AQERTs.

As our Search and Rescue mission continued, Regional Commander "Razar" and the DEF missionaires were attacked by Base Commander Bartzabel of the Old Empire Space Fleet: Mars Base. Battles in the space around Earth were frequent and intense.

In order to defend ourselves more effectively against attack, as indicated earlier, the DEF set up on underground base on the planet Venus, as a base of military operations. This was a well-hidden defensive position which gave us added strategic and logistical advantages, due to it's close proximity to the asteroid belt, which is our primary transport and communication installation at Space Station 33.

## MOSES ON THE MOUNTAIN

Active warfare continued between the BOTS and the DEF for more than 2,000 years, both in space and on Earth. Gradually, the well hidden and deeply entrenched forces of the "Old Empire" space fleet dwindled. Periodic reinforcements from the Domain Expeditionary Force, who use Space Station 33 as a jumping off point between galaxies, along their invasion route to targets much deeper into the galaxy, were recruited to assist in combat missions.

The forces of the BOTS were never replenished, or reinforced, because the very existence of the BOTS and the illegal prison planet operation were a carefully kept secret from the rest of the Old Empire. And, of course, the DEF destruction of their government seat at Canubis II, cut off their access to the resources of the Old Empire which is still largely untouched on the majority of planets amid the vast regions of the territory.

The DEF, while continuing to search for our lost battalion, overthrew the 3,000 year long domination of Egypt by the "divine" pharaohs who were placed in power by the BOTS.

The false façade civilization of Egypt lost much of it's influence over other civilizations in the area when the BOTS domination of the administrative side of Egypt was replaced with a new line of human Pharaohs in 2,040 BCE. The first human pharaoh moved the capital city of Egypt from Memphis to Heracleopolis.

Shortly thereafter, the battle continued on Earth between the BOTS forces as a war of religious conquest. Between 1500 BCE and about 1200 BCE, The Domain Forces attempted to teach the concept of an individual, Immortal Spiritual Being, to several influential beings in Egypt and the Near East.

One such instance resulted in a very tragic misunderstanding, misinterpretation and misapplication of the principle of All-Mother, as guided by Omnimat.

During the reign of the Egyptian Pharaohs, Amenhotep III and his son, Akhenaten. Their accomplice, Aquatic Unit Mission Specialist "Lemore", who inhabited the body of the beautiful history, Queen Nefertiti, succeeded in dismantling the power structure of the priest of Amun. After a brief success, they were ultimately assassinated by priests of the Old Empire following an intense battle in solar system space with the BOTS Mars fleet.

Ref: 1351 BCE through 1337 BCE -- (Earth Solar Date / Time 1228038.9849537 through 1233324.9849537)

In the aftermath of this ill-fated incursion, the "Old Empire" priests managed to corrupt the concept of individual immortality into the idea that there is only one, all-powerful IS-BE, and that no one else is or is allowed to be an IS-BE. Obviously, this is the work of the BOTS amnesia operation.

It is easy to teach this altered notion to beings who do not want to be responsible for their own lives. Slaves are such beings. As long as one chooses to assign responsibility for creation, existence and personal accountability for one's own thoughts and actions to others, one is a slave.

The principle of All-Mother was reinterpreted, by the BOTS priests, to mean that there is only one IS-BE, instead of the truth that everyone is an IS-BE! The religious systems resulting from the alteration demonstrate an utter unwillingness to take responsibility for one's own power as an IS-BE.

As a result, the concept of a benevolent, monotheistic IS-BE was adopted by many self-proclaimed prophets, such as the Egyptian slave leader -- Moses -- who grew up in the household of the Pharaoh Amenhotep III and his son, Akhenaten and his wife Nefertiti.

Our attempt to teach certain beings on Earth the truth that they are, themselves, an IS-BE, was part of a plan to overthrow the metaphorical, anthropomorphic panoply of gods created by the "Old Empire" mystery cult known to the DEF as "The Brothers of The Serpent". Their covert operations on Earth were known in Egypt as the Priests of Amun, the ancient, secret society who controlled all of the middle east region.

Unfortunately, Pharaoh Akhenaten, after generations of inbreeding of in the royal family, was not a very intelligent being, and was heavily influenced by self-glorification. He also altered the concept of the benevolent, individual spiritual being, introduced to him by Nefertiti. This simple concept was symbolized, as a sun god, Aten.

Our most dramatic victory, though temporary, was to move the capital city away from the stronghold of the BOTS priests of Amun, to a new location along the Nile. This location was plotted by the DEF as the precise geodetic center of the country of Egypt, as seen from space. Although the BOTS priests possessed knowledge of advanced astronomical geometry, it was never applied, except to further the prison planet agenda of the BOTS.

Although these strategic maneuvers were a short term blow to the power of the BOTS priests, the pitiful existence of Akhenaten was soon ended. He was assassinated by Maya and Parennefer, two of the Priests of Amun who represented the interests of the "Old Empire" forces.

As you know, the Christians still say "Amen" to unknowingly invoke the blessing of the Egyptian gods at the conclusion of each prayer. This is no doubt a residual affect have having been incarnated as Egyptians for hundreds of generations.

Aquatic Unit Mission Specialist "Lemore", who acted as co-regent, and wife the Pharaoh Akhenaten, was recalled to the DEF base, and the body of Nefertiti was secretly cremated. This was done to prevent detection of synthetic genetic material that was present in the body of the queen, should it ever be exhumed posthumously.

Subsequent to this failed plot, the DEF principle of All-Mother, under the guidance of Omnimat, was perpetuated by the Hebrew leader Moses while he was still in Egypt.

The Principle of All-Mother, inspired Moses to demand the freedom of the race of slaves who served the Pharaoh. All-Mother implies that every IS-BE have inherent right to autonomy. Emboldened by the guidance of Omnimat, he successfully led their escape from bondage.

Shortly thereafter Moses left Egypt with his adopted people, the Jewish people. Moses was able to coerce the new Pharaoh, through a series of events, which were, in part, affected remotely by the DEF missionaires, to free the slaves.

The explosion of the volcano on the island of Crete in the Mediterranean, home of the Minoans, was a coincidental disaster that affected the weather, the ocean, and land of Egypt adversely. Of course, Moses took advantage of this calamity to convince Pharaoh that "god" was working to defend his people.

Unfortunately, during their travels, while crossing the vast desert east of Egypt, Moses was intercepted by an operative of the BOTS near Mt. Sinai. With the aide of amnesia and mind-control mechanisms, Moses was tricked into believing that this operative was "the" One God.

Hypnotic commands, as well as technical and aesthetic tricks which are commonly used by the BOTS to trap IS-BEs, as well as heavy electronic force, were used against Moses to "convince" him that he was in direct communication with "the one god".

Of course, the version of the god implanted in the mind of Moses was the exact opposite of the *Omniscient and Omnipresent Matriarch*, a feminine entity of unlimited benevolence. The BOTS god, as a metaphorical version of the BOTS themselves, is a brutish, vindictive, patriarch! This purely obverse "god" concept demands unquestioning obedience and servitude to a vengeful "all-father".

Of course, the idea that an individual is an immortal spiritual being is forbidden! The BOTS indoctrinate all humans that they are solely and only a biological entity. Life is limited to the body, the race, the material possessions and the immediate survival for a single life-time.

As a further reassurance, the BOTS offered Moses a bribe: those who faithfully obeyed the "all-father" were assured that they were "the chosen ones". All others are "lesser beings", who are not favored by the "all-father", and were the enemies of the people. In order to keep this secret alliance with the BOTS hidden, the "faithful" must never intermarry, or allow others into the privileged inner circle. This is the same principle that binds the secret society of The Brothers of The Serpent into a closed circle of hatred, greed and power!

Likewise, no afterlife is possible, except to "return to the light" to enjoy a "heavenly" reward, perhaps, before being "judged" or treated at an AQERT. Thereafter, the slaves, who trusted the word of Moses implicitly, have worshiped a single god they call "Yaweh", which means "cannot be given a name".

In their own language, the name "Yaweh" means "anonymous". The BOTS operatives could not use an actual name or anything that would identify themselves, or blow the cover of the amnesia / prison operation. The last thing the covert amnesia / hypnosis / prison system wants to do is to reveal themselves openly to the IS-BEs on Earth. They feel that this would restore the inmates memories!

This is the primary reason that all traces of physical encounters between space civilizations and humans is very carefully hidden, disguised or denied.

This BOTS operatives "treated" Moses on the desert mountain top and indoctrinated him with "Ten Hypnotic Commands". These commands are very forcefully worded, and compel an IS-BE into utter subservience to the will of the operator. These hypnotic commands are still in effect and influence the thought patterns of millions of IS-BEs thousands of years later!

Incidentally, we later discovered that the BOTS operatives, or the so-called "Yaweh", provided Moses with an encoded text in the form of a small book of laws and mythology called the Torah. When it is read literally, or in its decoded form, the book will provide a great deal more false information to those who read it.

As with all of the religious mythology and philosophical misinformation laid down on Earth by the BOTS, one of the deadliest notions is the perverse concept of "only one". All prison planet philosophies incorporate the idea that a religious group is the "only one", that is, the "only" correct philosophy.

Naturally, this excludes and makes every other person and group an "enemy". Billions of people on Earth have murdered, and been murdered, over and over again, in the countless religious wars fought between opposing "only ones" on Earth. What better mechanism to promote warfare and chaos between the prison inmates than perpetual war between "only ones"?

Fortunately, the Vedic Hymns, which were delivered by The Domain Expeditionary Forces to Earth nearly 10,000 years earlier have survived in their basic ideological form. To the degree that the concept of an individual Eternal Spiritual Being, and the Benevolent Matriarch still exist on Earth, there is still a small hope that IS-BEs can regain their freedom.

The Veda is the source of nearly all Eastern religions and were the philosophical source of the ideas common to Buddha, Laozi, Zoroaster, and other philosophers.

They are the genesis of kindness and compassion on Earth. The civilizing influences of these philosophies could eventually replace the brutal idolatry of the "Old Empire", were it not for the continuing effects of the AQERTs surrounding Earth and the prison planet operation of the BOTS.

## PERIOD 4: A VICTORY

604 BCE China. -- Personnel Officer "Lor-el" and her team discovered a lost DEF officer whose IS-BE signature was very strong. After working with the officer through many lives on Earth he eventually came to inhabit the body of a man named Lao-Tzu. He was an official who worked as the Keeper of the Imperial Archives for the royal court of Zhou in China.

In The Domain, Lao-Tzu as known as the Independent Missionaire, "Lam-Mantra". As a member of the Lost Battalion, Lam-Mantra was an instructor and spiritual guide. It was through her efforts that the Hymns of The Veda were taught to human beings, and through memorizations by them, disseminated verbally through the East.

Lao-Tzu was reacquainted with *The Doctrine of The Eternally Benevolent Domain*, with the help of Lor-el. She re-learned how to control his own thoughts, recall her past life before Earth, and how to detect the influence of the BOTS.

In so doing, she ultimately overcame the effects of the "Old Empire" amnesia / hypnosis machinery and escaped from Earth. Before she departed, she wrote a summary of his spiritual wisdom, called the Tao Te Ching, which becomes the basis for Taoism. Of course, this is an abbreviated adaptation of The Way of All-Mother, translated into the local language.

His insights quickly spread to India, where the young Guatama Sakyamuni became a great teacher of The Way. Through the example of Lao-Tzu these understandings have been studied by other IS-BEs as a method to recover their freedom from the body.

A short excerpt of "The Way" of Lao-Tzu is as follows:

*"Without seeking, one may know all under heaven;*

*Without finding, one may know the way of heaven.*

*The wise man knows without searching,*

*Understands without thinking, accomplishes without acting.*

*To know when one does not understand is a virtue;*

*Failing to know that one does not understand is an error.*

*A wise man treats errors as errors.*

*He becomes more perfect each time an error is corrected.*

*Be honest with those who are honest. Also be honest*

*With those who are dishonest; thus is honesty attained.*

*All beings are basically benevolent. However, prevent those who do evil from harming others, for even they are basically benevolent.*

*What separates goodness and badness?*

*What difference is there between yes and no?*

*What distinguishes beauty and ugliness?*

*Front and rear join in the center.*

*Being and non-being are a circle of decision.*

*The way of heaven acts without competing,*

*Speaks little but answers well, is always present*

*Without being summoned, is not rushed but is well planned.*

*The wise man is skilled in all of his undertakings.*

*He who is skilled at counting needs no counting devices.*

*He who is fluid in speech needs no script to guide him.*

*A man of skill practices skill and conquers reality.*

*A man who fails to practice is conquered by failure to practice.*

*Walls form and support a room, yet the space between them is most important.*

*A pot is formed of clay, yet the space formed thereby is most useful.*

*Action is caused by the force of nothing on something, just as the nothing of spirit is the source of all forms.*

*One suffers great afflictions because one has a body.*
*Without a body what afflictions could one suffer?*
*When one cares more for the body than for his own spirit,*
*One becomes the body and looses The Way of The Spirit.*

*He who looks will not see it; he who listens will not hear it;*
*He who gropes will not grasp it.*
*The formless nonentity, the motionless source of motion.*
*The infinite essence of the spirit is the source of life; spirit is self.*

*The Self, the Spirit, creates illusion.*
*The delusion of Man is that reality is not an illusion.*
*One who creates illusions and makes them more real than reality,*
*follows the path of The Spirit and finds The Way of Heaven".*

The key ingredient to control and recovery of oneself as an IS-BE on Earth, as reported by Lao-Tzu, is to maintain strict mental discipline, so as not to be drawn into agreement with IS-BEs who value existence based the temporal, or sensational cravings of a body.

A body is merely a biologically engineered complex of interconnected cells, and genetic programs, including "epicenters" of artificial intelligence, each designed to control various involuntary stimulus-response activities, such as heart beat, blood flood, endocrine system functions, reproductive impulses, and so forth. All of these epicenters are unknowingly dominated and animated by the IS-BE, who is usually superior in power to the body. In the Easter world, these biological epicenters are called "chakras". In the Western world these epicenters are not observed. The epicenters behave as though they are IS-BEs, but they are not. Each "chakra" is merely a programmed set of biological mechanisms -- they have no sentient ability, or ability to act except as a response to stimuli.

In addition, artificial personalities or behavior circuits are usually interjected into the space of the IS-BE by the BOTS. These are used as remote control hypnotic control mechanisms to monitor and direct the behavior of individual IS-BEs on Earth. Just as a technician can send signals to a satellite in orbit around the planet to guide the speed and trajectory of the craft, so do the BOTS control the behavior of IS-BEs on Earth.

These behavior circuits, or hypnotic control points, are guided by simple, hidden control technology. However, when used with vicious intent by the BOTS, these simple mechanisms have a devastating affect over the thoughts and actions of IS-BEs inside the prison planet system.

An IS-BE attributes his or her bizarre, insane or erratic behavior to themselves and search endlessly to discover or rationalize the "meaning" or source of the unwanted thoughts that covertly control them. It is essential that every IS-BE be aware that any unwanted or undesirable thought, emotion, sensation, compulsion, sudden impulse, which is destructive to themselves or others, may have been carefully placed there by the BOTS as a hypnotic remote-control mechanism.

Loa-Tzu, supplied with this information by Lor-el, and trusting his own sanity and his inherent power to control his own thoughts was able, through careful observation and mental discipline, to segregate himself as an IS-BE from the hypnotic mechanisms of the BOTS. Thus, when departing from his body on Earth, he was able to avoid capture by the AQERTs long enough to return to the DEF.

## PERIOD 5: CYRUS, THE GREAT

576 BCE -- The IS-BE "signature" of Commanding Officer Aduk was now re-located to Persia. The Commanding Officer Aduk was incarnated as Cyrus II, the ruler of The Persian Empire who used the egalitarian methods of The Domain to conquer and unify the middle-east into the Persian Empire, the largest nation on Earth.

Herodotus, the Greek historian, claimed that when Cyrus was ten years old it was already obvious that Cyrus was not a lowly herdsman's son, stating that his behavior was too noble. In fact, the ruins of the now ancient civilization on Earth, Cyrus II is depicted in carved stone reliefs as a "winged god".

Airl contacted Commanding Officer Aduk telepathically. Along with the other missionaires, who disguised themselves as members of the imperial household, they each attempted, in various ways, to convince Cyrus II that he was once a member of the Domain by showing him pictures of Earth from space, spacecraft, and objects from his past in The Domain.

Their efforts at rekindling the memory of Commanding Officer Aduk were showing signs of success. However, after the death of his dearly loved wife, Cassandane, Cyrus was seduced by the sexual allure of the "mother goddess", the BOTS Lieutenant "Hathor", who inhabited the body of a daughter of the Median king Astyages. In her Earthly disguise, she drugged him, plied him with sensations of the flesh and gradually enticed him from The Way.

Shortly thereafter, in 530 BC, Cyrus was killed in battle along the Syr Darya River in modern-day Iran by an army led by Inspector Mastema. Once outside the body, Cyrus was picked up by the AQERT force screen, "treated" with the usual electric shock- amnesia-hypnosis mechanism and sent by Lieutenant "Hathor" to be reincarnated as a peasant farmer in India.

Stone statues of Cyrus II standing in the ruins of his once formidable empire, show him wearing a three-headed crown of serpents: the symbol that the BOTS controlled his mind, and tragically, his destiny on Earth.

After this, and similar failures to recover DEF personnel, Airl and her team reported back to the DEF Venus base. Incensed by this defeat, Airl requested, and was given permission from Regional Commander "Razar", who is in command of the DEF search and rescue mission, to assign a fighting force to seek out and attack the known BOTS installations.

## PERIOD 6: REINFORCEMENTS and RENAISSANCE

1135 - 1230 A.D. -- Regional Commander "Razar" requested reinforcements from The Domain Central Command. As a result, the war in the solar system space around Earth was intensified until the DEF, deploying two battle cruisers that were briefly diverted from their scheduled invasion route toward the center of this galaxy and beyond, gained the advantage.

Ordinarily, military resources that are already designated for specific assignments are not rerouted. However, since the DEF rescue mission was not a military mission, our resources at Space Station 33 were relatively limited. This misestimation, as mentioned earlier, contributed to the attack and capture of the DEF Himalaya Base.

So, special permission was granted by the Domain Central Invasion Command in Galaxy 3165 to provide reinforcement from The Domain Invasion Fleet before continuing with their normally scheduled duties.

Needless to say, within a few years after the arrival of the Domain battle cruisers, all of the remaining fleet of the Old Empire in Space Station 33, were located and destroyed by 1,230 A.D.

Since that time, Commandant Maalahk of the Prison Planet Earth: Mars Base, has been stranded with no military capability to attack the DEF any longer. However, the BOTS still possess their mind-control mechanism to use against Earth in the form their remaining impenetrable underground bases.

Nonetheless, this loss of strength lessened the influence of the BOTS in the region of Space Station 33. Without mobility and military force, their impact has diminished.

As a result, a "renaissance" of freedom and technology began to emerge on Earth as spiritual duress was reduced. IS-BEs, with less external influence than before, began to recall knowledge and Basic technologies that they knew from the ages past when they lived in technically advanced planets of the Old Empire before being captured and sent to Earth. By comparison to the history of humanity a virtual "explosion" of social and technical advancements appeared within only 500 years!

However, the fundamental situation on Earth remains the same you were briefed during your interviews with Airl in 1947:

*"The renaissance of invention on Earth that began in 1,250 AD with the destruction of the "Old Empire" space fleet in the solar system. Earth may have the potential to regain autonomy and independence, but only to the degree that humankind can apply the concentrated genius of the IS-BEs on Earth to solve the amnesia problem.*

*However, on a cautionary note, the inventive potential of the IS-BEs who have been exiled to this planet is severely compromised by the criminal elements of the Earth population.*

*Specifically, politicians, war-mongers and irresponsible physicists who create unlimited weapons such as nuclear bombs, chemicals, diseases and social chaos. These have the potential to extinguish all life forms on Earth, forever.*

*Even the relatively small explosions that were tested and used in the past two years on Earth have the potential to destroy all of life, if deployed in sufficient quantities. Larger weapons could consume all of the oxygen in the global atmosphere in a single explosion!*

*Therefore, the most fundamental problems that must be solved in order to ensure that Earth will not be destroyed by technology, are social and humanitarian problems. The scientific minds of Earth, in spite of mathematical or mechanical genius, have never addressed these problems.*

*Therefore, do not look to scientists to save Earth or the future of humanity. Any so-called "science" that is solely based on the paradigm that existence is composed only of energy and objects moving through space is not a science. Such beings utterly ignore the creative spark originated by an individual IS-BE and collective work of the IS-BEs who continually create the physical universe and all universes. Every science will remain relatively ineffective or destructive to the degree that it omits or devaluates the relative importance of the spiritual spark that ignites all of creation and life.*

*Unfortunately this ignorance has been very carefully and forcefully instilled in human beings by the "Old Empire" to ensure that IS-BEs on this planet will not be able to recover their innate ability to create space, energy, matter and time, or any other component part of universes. As long as awareness of the immortal, powerful, spiritual "self" is ignored, humanity will remain imprisoned until the day of its own, self-destruction and oblivion.*

*Do not rely on the dogma of physical sciences to master the fundamental forces of creation any more than you would trust the chanted incantations of an incense-burning shaman. The net result of both of these is entrapment and oblivion. Scientists pretend to observe, but they only suppose that they see, and call it fact. Like the blind man, a scientist can not learn to see until he realizes that he is blind. The "facts" of Earth science do not include the source of creation. They include only the result, or byproducts of creation.*

*The "facts" of science to not include any memory of the nearly infinite past experience of existence.*

*The essence of creation and existence cannot be found through the lens of a microscope or telescope or by any other measurement of the physical universe. One cannot comprehend the perfume of a flower or the pain felt by an abandoned lover with meters and calipers.*

*Everything you will ever know about the creative force and ability of a god can be found within you -- an Immortal Spiritual Being.*

*How can a blind man teach others to see the nearly infinite gradients that comprise the spectrum of light? The notion that one can understand the universe without understanding the nature of an IS-BE is as absurd as conceiving that an artist is a speck of paint on his own canvas. Or, that the lace on a ballet shoe is the choreographer's vision, or the grace of a dancer, or the electric excitement of opening night.*

*Study of the spirit has been booby-trapped by the thought control operation through religious superstitions they instill in the minds of men. Conversely, the study of the spirit and the mind have been prohibited by science which eliminates anything that is not measurable in the physical universe. Science is the religion of matter. It worships matter.*

*The paradigm of science is that creation is all, and the creator is nothing. Religion says the creator is all, and the creation is nothing. These two extremes are the bars of a prison cell. They prevent observation of all phenomenon as an interactive whole.*

*Study of creation without knowing the IS-BE, the source of creation, is futile. When you sail to the edge of a universe conceived by science, you fall off the end into an abyss of dark, dispassionate space and lifeless, unrelenting force. On Earth, you have been convinced that the oceans of the mind and spirit are filled with gruesome, ghoulish monsters that will eat you alive if you dare to venture beyond the breakwater of superstition.*

*The vested interest of the "Old Empire" prison system is to prevent you from looking at your own soul. They fear that you will see in your own memory the slave masters who keep you imprisoned. The prison is made of shadows in your mind. The shadows are made of lies, and pain, and loss, and fear.*

*The true geniuses of civilization are those IS-BEs who will enable other IS-BEs to recover their memory and regain self-realization and self-determination. This issue is not solved through enforcing moral regulation on behavior, or through the control of beings through mystery, faith, drugs, guns or any other dogma of a slave society. And certainly not through the use of electric shock and hypnotic commands!*

*The survival of Earth and every being on it depends on the ability to recover the memory of skills you have accrued through the trillenia; to recover the essence of yourself. Such an art, science, or technology has never been conceived in the "Old Empire". Otherwise, they would not have resorted to the "solution" that brought you to your current condition on Earth.*

*Neither has such technology ever been developed by The Domain. Until recently, the necessity of rehabilitating an IS-BE with amnesia has not been needed. Therefore, no one has ever worked on solving this problem. So far, unfortunately, The Domain has no solution to offer.*

*A few officers of The Domain Expeditionary Force have taken it upon themselves to provide technology to Earth during their off duty time. These officers leave their "doll" at the space station and, as an IS-BE, assume or take over a biological body on Earth. In some cases an officer can remain on duty while they inhabit and control other bodies at the same time.*

*This is a very dangerous and adventurous undertaking. It requires a very able IS-BE to accomplish such a mission, and return to base successfully. One officer who did this recently, while continuing to attend to his official duties, was known on Earth as the electronics inventor, Nicola Tesla.*

*It is my intention, although is not a part of my mission orders, to assist you in your efforts to advance scientific and humanitarian progress on Earth. My intention is to help other IS-BEs to help themselves. In order to solve the amnesia problem on Earth you will need much more advanced technology, as well as social stability to allow enough time for research and development of techniques to free the IS-BE from the body, and to free the mind of the IS-BE from amnesia.*

*Although The Domain has a long term interest in maintaining Earth as a useful planet, it has no particular interest in the human population of Earth, other than its own personnel here. We are interested in preventing destruction, as well as accelerating the development of technologies that will sustain the infrastructures of the global biosphere, hydrosphere and atmosphere."*

## PERIOD 7: DEF OFFICER TESLA

1856 A.D. -- A few officers of The Domain Expeditionary Force take it upon themselves to provide technology to Earth during their off duty time, on occasion. These officers leave their "doll" at the space station and, as an IS-BE, are born into or take over a biological body on Earth. In some cases an officer can remain on duty at the same time as they inhabit and control other bodies. However, this depends on the mental concentration required by the tasks to be performed.

This is a very dangerous and adventurous undertaking, to say the least. It requires a very able IS-BE to accomplish such a mission, and return to base successfully. One officer who did this recently, while continuing to attend to his official duties, entered into a body on 10 July, 1856, in the village of Smiljan, Vojna Krajina (today's Serbia). He was a boy named Nikola Tesla.

By April, 1884 Officer Tesla was in New York working with, and eventually competing against ,Thomas Edison. The project he worked on was to develop the first systems to supply electricity to Earth, as well as several other rudimentary technologies. Although Edison designed a workable, but cumbersome electric generator for direct current, Tesla completely redesigned the company's generators to deliver a much more efficient alternating current.

However, after Edison failed to pay Tesla for his work, Tesla quit and moved on to other ventures. He "invented" technologies that have existed throughout planetary systems in the physical universe for trillions of years, but which had never been allowed by the BOTS to appear on Earth.

These included the X-ray, wireless power transmission, and the radio. Of course, he also assembled a device he called the "Teslascope" in order to "communicate with extraterrestrials on the planet Venus" where he claims that he was "born". This was an obvious violation of DEF security protocol, but did not warrant disciplinary action because none of the IS-BEs on Earth believed that he actually came to Earth from Venus -- which he actually did, of course.

Tesla mentioned many times during his career that he thought his inventions such as his Tesla coil, used in the role of a "resonant receiver", could communicate with other planets. In 1896, Tesla told interviewers that the possibility of beckoning Martians was the extreme application of his principle of propagation of electric waves.

*Time Magazine's* July 20, 1931 issue, acknowledging Tesla's 75th birthday, he was quoted as saying: *"[I have conceived] a means that will make it possible for man to transmit energy in large amounts, thousands of horsepower, from one planet to another, absolutely regardless of distance. I think that nothing can be more important than interplanetary communication. It will certainly come some day and the certitude that there are other human beings in the universe, working, suffering, struggling, like ourselves, will produce a magic effect on Mankind and will form the foundation of a universal Brotherhood that will last as long as humanity itself."*

> (Narrative Comment: Brotherhood, indeed! Although this metaphorical sentiment is understood, being assimilated into The Eternally Benevolent Domain, under the guidance of Omnimat and All-Mother, is hardly a "brotherly" activity.)

Many of the innovations offered to the IS-BEs by Officer Tesla resulted in an evolutionary leap forward, which subsequently enabled other advancements in energy and communications technology. Progress in his endeavors were very awkward and tedious in that the majority of the parts and devices he needed had to be built by hand, one at a time! And, of course, his efforts to help the prisoners of Earth were fought and opposed at every turn by the influence of the BOTS.

Through their mind-control mechanisms and prison "guards", they successfully suppressed the most beneficial and powerful of his innovations, which was a generator, that he built and tested in Colorado. The device would provide free electricity, conducted through the atmosphere, to the entire planet! The banker, J.P. Morgan, who provided funding for the project had the entire device dismantled and destroyed when he learned that the enormous profits from fossil fuel sales would be eliminated. As always, on Earth, solutions based the <u>least</u> benefit for humanity prevail.

Recently, the same technology has been deployed, based on original Tesla plans, as a global military weapon using the combined force of billions of watts of electricity, directed into the upper atmosphere from multiple stations located around the world. The weapon is capable of causing vast destruction at specifically targeted locations, including earthquakes and tsunamis. Conversely, the mechanisms, when directed at individual IS-BEs, can used as a mind-control, or population control weapon.

Until the BOTS no longer control Earth, the efforts of The Eternally Benevolent Domain will be fought and undermined at ever turn, using the psychotic "leaders" of Earth as pawns in the game of eternal imprisonment.

## PERIOD 8: MARS, CYDONIA BASE

1914 A.D. -- During the spring another officer of the DEF was sent on a reconnaissance mission to Earth. His mission orders required that the officer inhabit the body of a member of the ruling House of Hapsburg in Austria. The purpose of the mission was to gather information about the current state of affairs. The nature of such a mission requires a very powerful IS-BE. One must enter into the atmosphere of Earth, knock out the IS-BE from the body one intends to inhabit, impersonate that individual convincingly, gather information without raising suspicion, and then return to base without incident.

The discovery of the BOTS base on Mars was made when the body of the Archduke of Austria, which had been taken over by Land Mission Specialist Rameth. He was not aware how much the Hapsburg Empire was hated by an insurgent faction in the region, so he is caught off guard when the body of the Archduke was assassinated by a Bosnian student.

Rameth was distracted, in an attempt to save the wife of the Archduke who had been shot just seconds before, and was "knocked out" of the body when his body was shot through the neck by the assassin. Momentarily disoriented outside the body, Rameth inadvertently penetrated an AQERT force screen. He was captured and instantly recognized by the BOTS as an officer of The Domain, due to his IS-BE "signature" and characteristic energy emanation of a high-powered IS-BE, which is not inherent on Earth.

As such, he was taken directly to Base Commander Bartzabel in an underground base 500 miles north of the equator of Mars, the Cydonia Region. Exhaustive attempts to "treat" Officer Rameth with shock and hypnosis failed to produce the desired effect of an IS-BE who can be placed in a body, in prison, on Earth.

In frustration, Officer Rameth was placed in an electronic prison cell at the Mars base by Inspector Mastema, hoping to use him as ransom, in exchange for the locations of the Domain bases.

After years of relentless Interrogation in captivity the plan proved useless. No ransom attempt was possible. For 27 years Officer Rameth remained "missing". The DEF could not detect his signature on Earth, or anywhere in the region of Space Station 33. So, nothing could be done except to wait.

One day in 1940, during a brief moment of lax security by the BOTS guards, Rameth escaped from the electronic "cell" and returned to the DEF base in the asteroid belt. He reported the incident, as well as the location of the BOTS base to Regional Commander "Razar".

Although the original mission of reconnaissance was not successful, the experience of Officer Rameth having a body killed, departing the body as an IS-BE, the disorientation that resulted in his capture, and subsequent attempts at "treatment" proved to be far more valuable information than a simple "news bulletin" about current affairs on Earth.

During the attempt to "treat" him, and observations made while he was incarcerated by the BOTS on Mars, Rameth revealed details of the process used by the BOTS that enabled them to use Earth as a "prison planet". Rameth also reported that the mechanisms for capturing IS-BEs in the region had been installed for a very long, perhaps millions of years.

This extraordinarily fortunate accident, observed and reported by a high powered Officer of the DEF proved to be the most valuable victory in our war against the BOTS to that time. The DEF could not have planned a more successful mission to infiltrate the BOTS operation at Space Station 33 if we had done it intentionally!

Based on this most valuable intelligence data, Regional Commander Razar dispatch a battle cruiser to the coordinates of the base provided by Rameth. The base was destroyed. The disintegrated ruins of pyramid structures, buildings and Pharaonic monuments on the surface of Mars remain visible today. The size of the underground base remains uncertain, as his ability to determine the entire extent of the BOTS base was limited to one specific location.

Although the surface base and some of the underground base were destroyed, it has become apparent, subsequently, that the influence of the BOTS base on Mars remain operational.

In retaliation for the attack on the Mars base, the DEF suspects that the events of World War on Earth were heavily influenced and accelerated by the covert mind-control mechanisms of the BOTS. The coincidental relaxation of security by the entire American military in Hawaii just days before the Japanese attack can not have occurred accidentally.

Likewise, the introduction of atomic fission weapons and rocketry technology to Earth at the same time cannot be a coincidence. It is apparent that the BOTS would rather destroy their own prison, rather than allow it to be discovered by the inmates!

Although it is not the mission of the DEF to intervene directly in the affairs of Earth, it is difficult, at best, to remain indifferent to the colossal cruelty and suffering being inflicted by the BOTS on the IS-BEs of Earth.

To the degree that several thousand DEF personnel are still captive on Earth, we can justify whatever measures are necessary to rescue them. However, this does not grant the DEF permission to violate mission orders or alter the established protocols of The Domain Expeditionary Forces.

## PERIOD 9: PRISON PLANET

1940 AD -- The official debrief filed by Land Mission Specialist Rameth regarding his captivity on Mars revealed that anyone who is not willing or able to submit to mindless economic, political and religious servitude as a tax-paying worker in the class system of the "Old Empire" are classified as "untouchable". They are sentenced to receive memory wipe-out and permanent imprisonment on Earth.

When the body of a human dies, and the IS-BE departs from the body, they are detected by an electronic "force screen", and captured. Then they are "treated" with an overwhelming electric shock which erases their memory. The IS-BE is ordered by hypnotic command to begin a "new life", that is, to take a body on Earth, and return to "base" at the end of their lifetime.

When the body of the IS-BE dies on Earth, an electronic force screen under the surface of Earth, called an AQERT (literally, "abode of the dead") recaptures them. At the AQERTs, the IS-BE is electric shocked and hypnotized to erase the memory of the life just lived, the IS-BE is immediately "commanded", hypnotically, to "report" back to Earth, as though they were on a secret mission, to inhabit a new body. Each IS-BE is told that they have a special purpose for being on Earth. But, of course the only purpose is to continue to remain in prison. Of course, the fact that Earth is a prison, is never mentioned or implied.

On the contrary, the fact is very thoroughly hidden from the inmates through the illusion created by very elaborate "false façade" civilizations, that they have "evolved" as a native species of animal on Earth. The absurdity of this notion, to any IS-BE who has not had their memory erased, demonstrates the overwhelmingly effectiveness the "treatment" methods.

The cycle of life-death-"treatment", life-death-"treatment", life-death-"treatment", life-death-"treatment", is repeated endlessly! To date, only a very few IS-BEs have escaped from this prison.

A cyclical repetition of human civilizations on Earth reflect the same pattern. Each civilization endures a brief lifetime, decays, dies and is resurrected. Every new body of civilization is killed, inevitably, by the social diseases, economic calamities, natural disasters, and military mayhem.

Each wave of death and rebirth is carefully attended by the BOTS to ensure a relentless decline. The same IS-BEs who built and ruined Rome, are the same IS-BEs who built and ruined Greece, and Mesopotamia and India in succession. The IS-BEs of Europe who were busily destroying each other and themselves in the Middle Ages, moved on to destroy the indigenous people of North America, who were already busy destroying themselves.

The diverse and divergent human population of Earth is an artificially enforced assembly of "untouchables" from a thousand planets and countless cultures. This caldron of conflicting cultures is stirred relentlessly by an unseen spoon. The BOTS sprinkle their brew of hopeless victims with generous doses of criminals vetted from the darkest depths of the "Old Empire". The prison guards unknowingly chant the ritual tune: "have faith and do what you're told to do".

Priest, politician / soldier, and banker, in unison, ensure that no lobsters escape from the boiling pot. If they try, they are pushed back down into the boiling bubbles of doom.

The Domain has never seen anything like this gruesome scene before. If our invasion plans ever take us to such a planet again, we avoid it like a deadly plague and place the entire region under quarantine! Or, simply eradicate the population.

## PERIOD 10: ROSWELL REVELATION

July, 1947 -- In response to the growing threat of global nuclear holocaust, promoted by the BOTS, the DEF sent a mission to Earth to avert this disaster. While surveying the area where intense experimental testing of atomic fission weapons was observed, Officer, Pilot and Engineer "Airl" and 3 other DEF personnel, were forced to crash land their craft near at Roswell, N.M. when it was struck by an intense discharge of lightning.

By coincidence, one of the humans who arrived at the rescue site had already been identified as one of the lost DEF battalion. Officer Airl was able to communicate telepathically with Adeet-Ren, who was a nurse at the 509th Bomb Group, at the Air Force base which deployed nuclear bombs over Hiroshima and Nagasaki, Japan one year earlier.

Airl conducted a series of interviews with Adeet-Ren, during which she reveals the existence of The Domain, and provides other information that Officer Airl thought appropriate to the time and circumstances.

The doll body Officer Airl used as a saucer pilot is "killed" with electric shock, by a psychiatrist, in an attempt to prevent her from unveiling the truth about Earth. Airl successfully escaped from the body and returns to the DEF base from which she continued her communication with Adeet-Ren.

The continuing communication between them over the intervening 62 years before her death at the age of 83 years, proved to be the principle therapy necessary to restore the memory and ability of Adeet-Ren, enabling her to return to active duty with the DEF.

This prolonged period of communication involved a great deal of intense and thorough reorientation and education for Adeet-Ren. This proved to be a milestone case study, as it were, from which our Medical Officer, "Raal-laam", was able to set up a "Rest-Care-Cure Unit" at the DEF base here in the asteroid belt. This is the first medical unit of this type in the history of the DEF, as no cases of severe amnesia have ever been encountered in The Domain.

Based on the successful rehabilitation through the communication with Officer Airl, Medical Officer Raal-laam prepared the briefing that you are studying now. We assume that continued communication, education and reorientation will eventual restore other lost DEF battalion member to active service.

However, as mentioned previously, the resources of this mission do not enable us to spend 60 years, or more, intensely communicating with each member of the lost battalion. If the rescue of one IS-BE requires this degree of time and effort to assure success, we will have to return to DEF Command Central, present our debrief and recommendations before we can return with a enough missionaires to do the job right.

---

**THIS CONCLUDES THE NARRATIVE OF DEBRIEF SECTION TWO: MISSION OPERATIONS MISSION 162589.32, GALAXY 3793**

# YOUR LIFE IN THE DEF

## DUTIES AND REGIMEN

Now that you have returned to active duty with the DEF, you will need to refresh and update your fundamental training. Also, you will reorient yourself to the duties and responsibilities of your post.

Fundamental training is composed of several parts:

1) Theoretical study of the principles of The Domain described fully in ***The Domain Directory of Policy and Procedure.*** The complete text and supplemental database are available at any communications station in this base. A complete contextual cross-reference, index, and tutorial are included for your convenience.

2) Practical Drills in application of principles you have studied in ***The Domain Directory of Policy and Procedure*** as they apply to real-time situations you are likely to encounter during the performance of your duties.

3) Policy and Procedure Training as regards the specific duties and responsibilities of your post.

4) Technical Skill enhancement for your post.

5) Training in Communication Procedures and Skills (required by DEF personnel, regardless of position or longevity).

Communication by telepathy is a skill and ability that must be practiced and perfected at all times. Without this essential ability, members of the DEF cannot operate as a cohesive unit. Practical application of your ability to send and receive communication is essential to the performance of your duties, whether on a space station, in space, on the surface of a planet, inside a body, or outside a body. To that end, your well-being as an IS-BE must be eternally acknowledged and nurtured for the benefit of yourself and The Domain.

6) Perception Sensitivity ( *NEW* ) is an essential ability, which, together with Communication, are fundamental to your performance as a member of the DEF.

As you have observed during your captivity on Earth, the inability to exit from a biological body, and reorient yourself in space and time as an IS-BE can have devastating consequences.

Your ability to transfer across space, permeate matter, inhabit life organisms, enter into and exit from the assorted mechanical bodies provided by the DEF to perform various functions, is of critical importance.

The DEF is developing new education and training methods, based on the successful rescue of several of the lost battalion personnel from Earth, for the benefit of all DEF personnel to prevent future disasters due to "mind-control" operations, such as that of the BOTS on Earth.

## LIFESTYLE AND LIBERTIES

While you are on duty, you will adhere to the schedule provided to you by your superior officer, or as required of all DEF personnel by the Commanding Officer, and perform the responsibilities of your post, as described in ***The Domain Directory of Policy and Procedure.***

During periods when your DEF duties and responsibilities do not require your attention, you are at liberty. Provided that you do not violate security protocols, as specified in ***The Domain Directory of Policy and Procedure***, you may come and go to and from the DEF base, and amuse yourself as you please.

*(**NOTE**: Due to the hazardous nature of the region of space surrounding Space Station 33, created by the BOTS, it is advised exercise extreme caution outside for force screens of the DEF base. This precaution has not ordinarily been required in the vast majority of galaxies and universe encountered by the DEF. As a safety precaution, please advise your superior officer if you intend to leave the DEF Base without escort, so that your position can be monitored.)*

### Quarters And Facilities

As on all DEF Mission bases, you are provided quarters for personal use. Quarters are assigned by the Quarter Master, according to the nature of your duties, as well as the necessities of your personal relaxation, rejuvenation, hygiene and physical attributes, if any. As you know, the DEF uses a limited number of what human beings would call "bodies" to perform a wide variety of duties in space, as well as inside the various DEF bases. These bodies are not biological entities, like those on Earth, which require elaborate environments to support them. Bodies used by the DEF are mechanical, primarily. A few are from species of life form that are most similar to insects on Earth, but much larger, of course.

In addition. this DEF installation is equipped with facilities for your pleasure and enjoyment:

**The Imaginearium**

This facility is a space in which you are free to create. Of course, the spiritual creation of your own space and universe does not require a pre-existing space or location. However, should you desire to create any objects or illusions within the confines of predetermined spatial dimensions, the Imaginearium is at your disposal.

An assortment of the most popular creative devices are available for your use, including:

- holographic generators
- concept design stimulators
- sensation emulators
- life form construction kits
- universe diversification puzzles

- tools of destruction
- force field emitters
- light illusion wands
- interdimensional travel simulators
- environment generators

You will discover that the Imaginearium is a frequent gathering place for off-duty interaction between members of the DEF.

**The Lounge**

The Lounge is an ambient environment for social interaction with other members of the DEF. This space provides a wide variety of amusements, games, picture shows and social activities for communication between DEF personnel.

***NOTE**: Since IS-BEs do not require energy infusion from an exterior source, such as are required by biological bodies, or mechanical units, this base is not supplied with any provisions such as atmosphere, solid food, liquid nutrients. There is a generous store of various chemical compounds and gases available, if needed.*

**The Archive**

The archive is an extensive database of information about all of the galactic and extra-galactic possessions of The Domain. This includes every documented piece of information gathered, to date, from all over the vast regions of The Domain. The Archive contains all of the photographic, holographic, text, audio (where applicable), data and sensual perceptions gleaned from the spaces visited or acquired by The Domain Expeditionary Force.

### Vehicles and Excursions

A limited number of vehicles, unusually scout craft, are available for use by authorized Pilots of the DEF. Sightseeing excursions are often organized by members of the DEF. If you would like to participate in an excursion, please indicate your desire to be advised of the excursion schedule. Excursions are first come, first serve, and are limited to the number of bodies accommodated by the craft being deployed.

*(**NOTE**: As vehicles require the use of mechanical bodies for power and navigation, you must be authorized to occupy and operate the body type required by the vehicle being used. Typically, a Class III doll body, is the minimum requirement.)*

**WE CREATE THE ETERNALLY BENEVOLENT DOMAIN!**

# THE DOMAIN ANNEXATION OF EARTH

The Domain Expeditionary Force Invasion Timetable is currently scheduled for Annexation of Space Station 33, including all objects and space within the solar gravitational force of Sun 12. This will include the planet Earth. The specific Earth date and time is restricted information, of course, known only to the DEF Missionaires who will carry out the applicable orders.

However, it can be safely assumed that The Annexation will occur in less than One Mission Cycle from this date.

To be more precise, "annexation" is defined, in the language of North American English, as follows:

- ***noun***: the formal act of acquiring something (especially territory) by conquest or occupation

  ***Example:*** *"The French annexation of Madagascar as a colony in 1896"*

In the case of Earth, specifically, Annexation is the action of including IS-BEs and their respective universes, as part of The Eternally Benevolent Domain, as dictated by the "***Declaration of Eternal Benevolence***", as follows:

1. *The Goal of The Eternally Benevolent Domain is to unite all immortal spiritual beings, space, energy and possessions to form a vast, multi-dimensional civilization guided by the transcendent principle of All-Mother, under*

*the supervision of The Omniscient and Omnipotent Matriarch.*

2. *The Duty of The Omniscient and Omnipotent Matriarch is to supervise the convergence and integration of all co-created universes into a unified multidimensional civilization based on the principle of All-Mother.*
3. *The Purpose of The Omniscient and Omnipotent Matriarch is to provide the volition and guidance to coordinate The Plan to create order and suppresses chaos for all beings who coexist as The Eternally Benevolent Domain, according to the principle of All-Mother.*
4. *The Plan delineates our collective action toward realizing The Goal, as dictated by The Omniscient and Omnipotent Matriarch and fulfilled by the IS-BEs who comprise The Eternally Benevolent Domain.*
5. *The Activity is guided and unified into a cooperative endeavor by The Omniscient and Omnipotent Matriarch to nurture and defend all beings whose intentions and actions demonstrate a will to persist as a cooperative and productive member of The Eternally Benevolent Domain.*

These provisions, with emphasis on # 5 above, are the criteria that will determine whether or not any specific IS-BE will be included in the Annexation process. Likewise, this presumes that the IS-BE possesses the ability to participate in The Domain.

# CONCLUSION

**Due to the nature of the Search and Rescue, as described in the foregoing debrief of DEF INVASION MISSION 162589.32, GALAXY 3793, orders have been received that this mission is to be terminated by DEF Command Central.**

**All mission personnel are to be recalled to Domain Expeditionary Force Home Base, effective Solar Time / Date:**

**11 December, 2050.**

**Based on further research and evaluation conducted by the Evaluation and Authorization Unit of DEF Command Central, new mission orders may be ordered, and personnel assigned in accordance with resource allocations available, as provided by the DEF Invasion Master Plan.**

**Routine communication and security personnel stationed at Space Station 33 will remain to continue their assigned duties, as specified by DEF Command Central.**

**Any DEF personnel who have not yet been rescued are encouraged to contact DEF Mission 162589.32 immediately. Contact can be established in the following ways:**

**1) By telepathic communication with any DEF personnel**

**2) Internet communication message sent to the following address: defbase33co07@gmail.com**

# PERSONAL NOTE FROM ADEET- REN

*I received permission to send you a personal note at the end of this transmission. The last letter I sent to you, from Earth, before I returned to The Domain was my personal request to publish the transcripts of my interviews with Airl from 1947.*

*I know that must have been a difficult and dangerous decision for you to make. Thank you for your understanding that the well-being of all IS-BEs would be served by doing this.*

*I can assure you, and advise you, that The Domain is doing everything it can to recover all of the lost members of the battalion that has been incarcerated on Earth for the last 10,000 years. Even though we are leaving soon to return to DEF Central Command, I am sure that the situation will be reevaluated and new orders will be issued.*

*If and when a new mission is dispatched to Earth with the resources needed to destroy the AQERTs, undo the effects of amnesia and hypnosis laid in against the DEF personnel, I am confident that you will be among the first to be rescued.*

*As you know there are still more than 2,800 members of the DEF remaining on Earth. We know that they are DEF members because there IS-BE "signature" is fundamentally different than that of IS-BEs who came to Earth from other regions in the physical universe. DEF personnel are not native to the physical universe, and as such do not have the same characteristics.*

*This distinguishing feature make it possible for the DEF to know who they are. We also know where they are located currently.*

*However, help is still needed from you. IS-BEs from The Domain are probably aware, to a greater or lesser degree, that they are "different". They have some degree of awareness that "something" is going on, and that the illusions of "reality" on Earth are not what they appear to be.*

*Some of the members of the lost DEF battalion actually serve rudimentary functions at our communications installation in the asteroid belt, while at the same time, continuing to occupy bodies on Earth. The are partially, but not "analytically", aware of this dichotomy. This is due to the fact than an IS-BE is not a physical entity, and is not bound to any specific location in space or time.*

*Therefore, an IS-BE is capable of inhabiting more than one body, doing more than one function, or having multiple identities, simultaneously. This complex puzzle is compounded by the bizarre nature of the BOTS amnesia / hypnosis operation. They has created a very unique situation, never before encountered in the history of the DEF.*

*Any communication we can deliver, in any form, through any means, may help the members of the lost battalion, and others, regain their memory. When the DEF does return, whether as a new rescue mission, or when the Annexation Mission arrives at Space Station 33, the matter will be resolved one way or another. However, in Earth years, this could be a very long time in the future. Perhaps as long as 5,000 years.*

*Unfortunately, it is highly doubtful that the current prison population of Earth will remain stable for very long. We know with certainty that planet Earth is very unstable and highly volatile as an environment for life forms. Environmental cataclysm and catastrophe are normal on Earth.*

*In addition, we are sure that it is only a matter of time, a very brief time, before social / economic disaster -- provoked by the BOTS -- will disable or reverse the technological advances of the past 100 years and make our efforts to keep track of our personnel more difficult.*

*Human beings will be enslaved physically and economically by the BOTS, and the amnesia / mind-control mechanism will remain in force until methods of undoing the damage are developed. This is not a task that has ever been encountered or necessitated in the history of this universe, as far as the DEF knows. It has certainly never been a problem in The Eternally Benevolent Domain where IS-BEs are fully aware, functional, and able to communicate with each other as spiritual beings!*

*I can assure you that The DEF will return. However, it may not be soon enough to rescue the IS-BEs who we have failed to salvage so far, despite thousands of years of relentless effort.*

*We have made progress, destroying the BOTS space fleet and the Mars base. However, the prison planet remains. Ordinarily, The Domain would have not even have an interest in trying to rescue IS-BEs from a prison planet, regardless of the overwhelming injustices that brought the majority of beings to Earth. The Domain Invasion Time Table is not intended to rescue anyone.*

*Indeed, it is not inconceivable that the planet will be "cleansed" of life forms, in preparation for use by The Domain for other purposes. Or, the planet could be cleansed of only selected life forms (which often occurs). Since human beings consume vast resources to sustain their bodies, they are highly destructive. Therefore, they will be the first to go. Plants and trees are often left intact, while others are eliminated. It is simple matter of economy and aesthetics.*

*It is more likely that the BOTS and their AQERTs will be destroyed completely by an overwhelming use of force. The entire region of space, including Earth, will be "cleansed". In this case, the IS-BEs who inhabit biological bodies on Earth will be "released".*

*Since they are immortal, they will continue to be immortal. Nothing will ever change this. Eventually, these may or may not be absorbed into The Domain, as described in the debrief. It is not the responsibility of The Domain to rehabilitate IS-BEs. Each one will create The Eternally Benevolent Domain, or remain isolated in a state of eternal oblivion, accordingly.*

*The fact is that the physical universe is a very, very big place. The Domain itself is vast, and unbounded -- beyond physical universe rules or dimensions. There are trillions of trillions of IS-*

*BEs in the physical universe who can be very easily incorporated into The Eternally Benevolent Domain, and the principle of All-Mother.*

*By contrast, the average IS-BE on Earth is highly disabled, and difficult -- if not impossible -- to communicate with because they are already at the lowest end of the physical hierarchy of biological bodies. And, spiritually, they have become virtually "untouchable", due to the brutality of the BOTS.*

*Yet, in spite of these overwhelming circumstances there is hope. Every IS-BE will be embraced into The Eternally Benevolent Domain eventually. Omnimat and All-Mother are irrepressible and all-inclusive. As spiritual entities, we are all fundamentally inseparable. Ultimately, we are All-Mother.*

*As long as you remain on Earth do not take the affairs of humankind too seriously. Do not become overly interested in the microcosmic events and dramatic illusions of "reality". On Earth, nearly everything is a lie, or delusion, intended to distract you or direct your attention inward, into the prison, into false games of false civilizations, inside the walls of the prison.*

*Remember who you are. The physical universe is a cloud floating across the sky on a spring day. The aesthetic allure one could assign to this fluffy vapor, does not change the fact that is merely a collection of molecules suspended in a space, created by IS-BEs, and sustained by the agreement of IS-BEs.*

*Remember who you really are. You are the source of creation. You create your own universe. Help as many others as possible to remember that they are also Immortal Spiritual Beings. In the words of Shalnam-Aran, the* Way of All-Mother *is The Way of The Spirit:*

*"The Self, the Spirit, creates illusion.*
*The delusion of Beings is that All is not an illusion.*
*One creates illusions, enjoying, renewing, destroying.*
*Creation and Joy are The Way of All-Mother."*

You must remain aware of your spiritual self, or risk not being detected by the 'tree of life' if the DEF returns to find you. Recognize the influences of the BOTS. Avoid their traps. Fight their lies with truth. Communicate with IS-BEs as an IS-BE. Be who you really are and expect others to be also. Be constantly vigilant. The Eternally Benevolent Domain is already here. We will remain in communication with you as long as you remain in communication with us.

I am present, as Omnimat is present, in the eternal now.

Yours In All-Mother,

Adeet-Ren (Matilda)

**WE CREATE THE ETERNALLY BENEVOLENT DOMAIN!**

END OF TRANSMISSION

---

# INDEX

1351 BCE, 186

509th Bomb Group, 7

*aesthetic pain*, 90
*Ahura Mazda*, 79, 134
Akhenaten, 186
Amenhotep, 186
*amnesia*, 5, 186, 190, 202, 206, 207
*ancient*, 78, 134, 187
*Annunaki*, 135
*Aquatic Unit*, 134
Army Air Force, 7

*Babylon*, 5
*bacteria*, 91
*Battalion*, 78, 133
*biological*, 5, 57, 89, 92, 207
*body*, 78, 89, 90, 91, 92, 134, 207
Brothers of The Serpent, 187
Buddha, 192

*chemical-electrical trigger*, 89
*civilization*, 79, 134, 206
*cyclical stimulus-response generators*, 89

*dogma of physical sciences*, 204
*Domain Expeditionary Force*, 7
*Domain Search Party*, 135

*Earth*, 5, 7, 57, 78, 133, 134, 185, 187, 190, 202, 203, 204, 205, 206, 207
*economic*, 90, 141
*Egypt*, 5, 187, 188
English language, 57
*evolution*, 92

*false civilizations*, 5
*faravahar*, 79, 134
*flesh bodies*, 89, 90, 91, 92
*freedom*, 93

*galaxy*, 140
god, 186, 187, 190, 204
*gods*, 79, 134, 187
*government*, 140
*gravity*, 91
*Greece*, 5

heavy gravity, 57
*Himalayas*, 7
*homo sapiens*, 135
hypnotic commands, 189, 191, 206

idolatry, 192
*immortal*, 204
*India*, 5
*insignia*, 91
*IS-BE*, 5, 7, 78, 89, 90, 92, 93, 134, 186, 187, 189, 190, 202, 203, 204, 205, 206, 207

Jewish slaves, 188

Laozi, 192
*lost Battalion*, 133, 135

*military*, 91
*mind*, 205, 206, 207
Moses, 186, 188, 190
Mt. Sinai, 189

Nefertiti, 186
*Nephilim*, 135
*Nicola Tesla*, 207

*Oannes*, 134
*Old Empire*, 5, 90, 93, 140, 186, 187, 192, 202, 203, 206

*paradigm*, 203, 205
Pharaoh, 186, 187
planet, 57, 140, 202, 204, 207
*political*, 90, 140
*power*, 79, 90, 92, 134, 186
Priests of Amun, 187
*prison*, 7, 190, 205, 206
*proof*, 7

radiation, 57, 91
*religion*, 205
*remote control*, 91
*renaissance*, 202
responsibility, 186
Roswell, 7

*science*, 203, 204, 205, 206
*scientific*, 203, 207
secret, 187
*sexual reproduction*, 89
*slave masters*, 206
*slaves*, 93, 190
*soldier class*, 91
*soul*, 206
*space craft*, 79, 90, 92, 134
*spectrum*, 91, 205
*Sumerians*, 135
*Sun Type 12, Class 7*, 5, 57
*superstition*, 205
*survival*, 206

*The Domain*, 7, 78, 79, 89, 90, 92, 93, 133, 134, 135, 141, 185, 206, 207
*The Domain travel trillions of*, 92
*tree of life*, 78, 134
*trillions*, 5, 93
Tutankhamen, 186

*universe*, 5, **33**, 89, 92, 203, 204, 205

Vedic Hymns, 192

*wavelength*, 78, 89, 133

Yaweh, 190, 191

Zoroaster, 192